A rap on the window sent Dana's already racing heart into overdrive

She jerked up and saw Patrick leaning down, peering into the car, a frown on his face.

She inched the glass down just enough. "Don't you have a meeting to finish?" she snapped.

Patrick's expression dissolve... opened his mouth... maybe? She didn't... he was going to sa...

"I'm sorry." He jamm... ...his... ...he pockets of his jeans. Dana w... ...n't notice how well those jeans fitted. I know you were hoping for a better outcome from the school board meeting."

"I was hoping... Oh, never mind."

"Can—this is ridiculous. Can you get out of the car? I only have a minute or so, and this is giving me a crick in my neck."

"Good, because you've been a total pain in my neck. Why did you completely waste my time?" She clenched her hands around the steering wheel.

"Come on. Two minutes—that's all I have and all I'm asking for." Patrick cocked his head to one side. "Please?"

What could he say in two minutes that would change anything? But what was the harm in wasting another two minutes? "Oh, okay." Dana reached for the door handle, hating to give in.

She'd have to watch herself around Patrick Connor.

Dear Reader,

As a former teacher, I feel at home in most any part of a school—except when it comes to the school clinic. Beyond handing out a bandage and a hug, I would be at a loss if called upon to do the quick two-step most school nurses are asked to do on a daily basis.

In this day and age of shrinking school budgets, these ladies (and gentlemen) are called upon to be resourceful and caring—and to have a sense of humor about mishaps and mistakes. What better sort of woman could I choose for my heroine?

In fact, it was seeing the deft juggling act of my local elementary-school nurse that inspired me. Her story isn't Dana's story, and the school in this book isn't patterned after any one school, but I hope I got enough of the flavor right so that readers can see how a school nurse has more to do than hand out those aforementioned bandages and hugs, especially when love enters the picture!

I hope you enjoy Dana and Patrick's story. Let me know via my Web site, www.cynthiareese.net.

Sincerely,

Cynthia Reese

FOR THE SAKE OF THE CHILDREN

Cynthia Reese

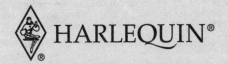

HARLEQUIN®

TORONTO • NEW YORK • LONDON
AMSTERDAM • PARIS • SYDNEY • HAMBURG
STOCKHOLM • ATHENS • TOKYO • MILAN • MADRID
PRAGUE • WARSAW • BUDAPEST • AUCKLAND

Recycling programs
for this product may
not exist in your area.

ISBN-13: 978-0-373-71533-6
ISBN-10:   0-373-71533-1

FOR THE SAKE OF THE CHILDREN

ABOUT THE AUTHOR

Cynthia Reese lives with her husband and their daughter in south Georgia, along with their two dogs, three cats and however many strays show up for morning muster. She has been scribbling since she was knee-high to a grasshopper and reading even before that. A former journalist, teacher and college English instructor, she also enjoys cooking, traveling and photography when she gets the chance. *For the Sake of the Children* is her fourth book.

Books by Cynthia Reese

HARLEQUIN SUPERROMANCE
1415–THE BABY WAIT
1451–WHERE LOVE GROWS
1507–NOT ON HER OWN

Don't miss any of our special offers. Write to us at the following address for information on our newest releases.

Harlequin Reader Service
U.S.: 3010 Walden Ave., P.O. Box 1325, Buffalo, NY 14269
Canadian: P.O. Box 609, Fort Erie, Ont. L2A 5X3

In memory of Mama Clyde,
whom I miss most fiercely.

Acknowledgments:

I owe so much in the way of guidance,
ideas and vision to my editor Victoria Curran,
to Wanda Ottewell and to Megan Long.
They had ideas about this project that gave it an
entirely new direction and made me grow as a
writer. I'd also like to thank my sister, Donna,
for helping me through the rough patches, and
my critique partners, Tawna Fenske, Cindy Miles,
Stephanie Bose and Nelsa Roberto.

Thanks also to fabulous real school nurse
Laura White and her nurse friends
who helped me along—all errors are mine!

CHAPTER ONE

THE CRANKY SCHOOL BUS GEARS ground out a protest as Patrick Connor pedaled the clutch and tried to coax the transmission into shifting.

I had to be out of my ever-lovin' mind—

"Fight! Fight!"

The words any school-bus driver dreads hearing ricocheted off the curved ceiling of the bus. Patrick's gaze shot to the wide rearview mirror to confirm his worst fear.

Yep. There it was, the telltale circle of excited onlookers, forming a protective fence around the combatants.

Patrick groaned and pulled the bus next to the curb.

On his first day—and last, if he had any say in it—of driving a school bus, he indeed had a fight on his hands.

At the next board meeting I'm voting for a raise for these bus drivers. With that in mind, he swung himself out of the seat and marched through the pack of students.

The kids reluctantly gave way then drifted back to their seats. Patrick shoved aside the remaining stragglers between him and the combatants to see two boys, their fists flying.

"Take it back!" one boy screamed at the other as he pummeled him. "Take it *back!*"

Patrick remembered what it was like to be ten and have your honor on the line. He remembered how fast and hot the adrenaline coursed through your veins, how you either stood up and declared your manhood—well, prepubescent boyhood—or were assigned the status of wuss.

Still, such pressure didn't change the fact that the bus was already ten minutes behind schedule. Making the situation even worse was that the school was in sight. Five more minutes, and those kids would have been somebody else's problem.

"Okay, fellas. Break it up." He yanked the two boys apart and stood between them. A quick check told him that one would be sporting a shiner and the other would have the honor of a split lip and a nosebleed all over his shirt.

What do I do now?

Both the boys were panting like Thoroughbreds at the starting gate. If he stepped from between them in order to make that five-minute trip to school, they'd be at each other's throats again.

But, dang it, he was ten minutes late already.

"Royce started it, Mr. Connor," a kid sitting in a nearby seat told him.

The comment initiated a volley of protests from all sides. Patrick came to a decision and guided the boys to the front of the bus, when he evicted the small fry currently occupying the seats.

"You—there." He indicated that Royce should assume one of the seats. "And you," he said to the other kid, who looked like a Holmes boy. "Over there. We have five minutes—*five minutes*—to get us parked and y'all into school. I don't want to hear a peep from anybody."

Patrick more or less held his breath for much of the five minutes left of the bus ride.

He drew up to a stop in front of the old school that

pretty much appeared as it had back when he'd attended. The air brakes whooshed as he set them, and he sat for a moment longer, not daring to remove his hands from the wheel for fear that the students would notice his fingers trembling.

Then he turned slowly and opened the bus doors. He aimed a warning glance at Royce as the kid bounced up, intent on slipping past him.

"Don't even think about it," Patrick growled.

The other students filed past, rubbernecking at Royce's bloody shirt and the Holmes kid's eye, which was puffing up like phyllo dough. One little girl in braids and glasses stopped short at Patrick.

"Mr. Connor, you shoulda put 'em in their usual seats. Mr. Willie makes 'em sit in assigned seats. That way, he can keep an eye on 'em."

She was giving him an eyeful of pity. Now Patrick felt like a total screwup.

"Well, um, thanks, Bridget. It is Bridget, right?" At her nod and smile, he added, "Next time I'll do that."

Her gap-toothed smile grew wider. "Don't worry. My mom says new things need lots of practice."

This old dog won't be practicing any more new tricks. But he didn't want to dash the little girl's hopes that he wasn't the wimp she feared, so he settled for a nod.

Driving the bus had seemed the perfect solution to the transportation crisis. Vann Hobbes, the school superintendent and his best friend, had mentioned the previous afternoon that the regular driver had to be out for a doctor's appointment. Vann had found no takers on the list of substitute drivers.

"I'll do it," Patrick had told his buddy. "I've got a license to drive a commercial vehicle. Tell me the route, and I'll do it for you."

"You? Drive a bus?"

"Why not? At least all my troubles will be behind me," Patrick had joked.

Boy, had he been dreaming.

Now Patrick squared his shoulders and rose from his seat. With a glower, he silenced Royce's wailing and trekked from seat to seat, ensuring everyone was off the bus.

Halfway back, he spotted a powder-puff pink shirt and blue jeans with girly little bows. The child was wrapped into a tight fetal position. His breath caught as he zeroed in on dark silky hair and flushed cheeks.

Annabelle.

But of course it wasn't Annabelle. Gulping down the lump in his throat, Patrick knelt in the aisle. Tentatively, he reached out a hand, then drew back.

He studied the little girl for a long moment, drinking in the innocence of her face, the way her black eyelashes fanned out against her cheeks, how her tiny pink mouth sucked on a forbidden thumb. She couldn't be more than four or so, probably in pre-kindergarten. Healthy. Whole. Alive.

"Hey, you! That was the tardy bell! Can I go now?"

Royce's voice boomed through the interior of the bus, shaking Patrick loose from the spell he was under. He gritted his teeth and put his hand on the little girl's shoulder. She was too damn young to be in school. She should have been outside running and playing, not stuck inside somewhere.

The little girl yawned and stretched. "But I'm tired, Mommy," she protested, still half-asleep.

"You're at school, honey," Patrick said. "It's time to go in. Who's your teacher?" he asked.

Brown eyes—thank God they were brown and not

blue like Annabelle's—rounded in panic. Then the panic subsided and she nodded. "Miss Elephant."

Patrick raised his eyebrows. "Miss Elephant?" He considered the list of pre-K teachers. "Oh, you mean Miss Ellison?"

"That's what I said," the little girl told him, sweeping by him in the grand manner of a queen. "Miss Elephant."

Patrick got up on creaky ankles and knees and watched her go.

He checked the rest of the seats. The bus was empty save for the two defiant, sulking boys. Patrick shepherded them down the steps.

"We gotta go to the office? So what?" Royce mouthed off. "All the principal's gonna do is suspend me from taking the bus for a week. Fine by me. That way I won't have to put up with dorks like him."

The Holmes kid bristled anew. For a second, Patrick thought the two would go at it again.

Jack Harrison, the principal, came out on the sidewalk, a petulant expression on his face. "Do you realize you're ten minutes late?" he said. "Ten minutes! And some of the students were telling me there was a fight!"

Patrick swallowed a retort and presented the two boys to Harrison. "They're all yours. Don't know what it was about, but I expect you can sort it out."

Harrison stepped back and peered at the students' faces. "Good Lord! Well, don't just stand there! They need medical attention. That one has started bleeding from the nose."

Patrick didn't bother suppressing a roll of his eyes. "C'mon, fellas. Appears you get to visit the school nurse."

"See?" Royce said in a singsong voice. "Told you we wouldn't get in trouble."

"Now, that's where you're wrong," Patrick replied. "Because I'm not just a substitute bus driver. I happen to be chairman of the board of education, and I can make certain that you, mister, won't have to put up with other students for just a week. I'm thinking a month's suspension from the bus. Nah. Two. Nah. Maybe for the rest of the year."

The fight went out of Royce. "Oh, man," he moaned. "My mom is gonna kill me."

Patrick was sure he saw begging in the Holmes kid's eyes. Satisfied that he had the boys' attention, he pointed them toward the nurse's office. "Time to visit the new school nurse. Good thing for you two Nurse Nellie had to retire. Hope the new one doesn't have any more of that stinging antiseptic Nurse Nellie liked so much."

To be an octopus!

Dana Wilson pushed aside the thought and pressed into service the only two arms the Lord had seen fit to give her.

"Here, Ritalin for you," she said, edging a pill cup over to a rail-thin kid, "and a lovely dose of Zithromax for you." The liquid sloshed in the cup as she handed it to a pint-size girl with dreadlocks.

"You're not supposed to be saying what we take," the older kid admonished. "It's the law or something. We're not even s'posed to be in here at the same time. Our old nurse handed out meds to us one at a time."

Dana quashed a snort of incredulity. Of course she knew that. But try holding back a wave of kids. No thanks to the prankster who had locked her out of her clinic this morning, she was doing well to get the right pills in the right squirmy little bodies before those bodies zipped off to class.

Now, why am I putting up with this? Oh, yes. Kate. One beautiful blue-eyed angel baby—although I can't call a three-year-old a baby anymore.

Dana's line of kids waiting for morning meds stretched out the door and down the hall. Well, *waiting* might create the wrong impression. They shuffled, fidgeted, jostled one another, picked at the staples on the poster of a big laminated hand exhorting them to lend health a hand by actually washing their own hands.

If Dana didn't get them out of her little clinic soon, they'd be late for class and she wouldn't have a staple left on that bulletin board.

"Hey! Cut it out! Leave those staples alone!" she yelled as she noticed one kid steadily slipping a fingernail under an already loosened staple. The gesture of the newly positioned middle finger wasn't difficult to discover. Of course, she could be wrong. This only her third week at the school. She was still getting over how many kids needed morning meds after the school-issued breakfast.

The Ritalin and Zithromax dispatched, Dana called out, "Next!"

But before any other patients could step up to her counter, a man rounded the door and stopped short at the line.

"Whoa. We got an epidemic I don't know about?" he inquired.

Dana couldn't remove her eyes from his face. How absurd, plain absurd, to focus on a man's face to the point when you could look nowhere else. But the last place she expected to find a man that handsome was in a small-town elementary school. With his silvered dark hair, movie-star white teeth and intense blue eyes, he had a face made for a cologne ad.

His voice, though, held a south Georgia twang and his clothes—khakis and a worn chambray work shirt with some sort of logo on it—tagged him as a native of Logan.

A parent? A teacher? The guy did have two kids by the scruff of the neck.

"Oh, my gracious! What happened?" Dana had managed to take her eyes off his face long enough to see obvious injuries. "Bring them on in and I'll have a look."

In quick order, she had a pack of ice on the little kid's eye—Mike Holmes, he'd said his name was—and was tilting the bigger, surlier boy's head forward, ordering him to pinch his nostrils together.

Only then did she dare return her gaze to the man who'd brought the two boys in.

She found his dark blue eyes assessing her with more than a little interest. At her regard, he spoke up. "They got into a fight on the bus."

A bus driver? Man, oh, man, she wished they'd had bus drivers like this when she was in school. But no, she'd had all the oogy ones.

Dana yanked her brain back from its descent into a hormone lovefest. Marty had been that good-looking in his own way, and when the going had gotten tough, her ex-husband had run as though demons were after him. So why imbue a guy with wisdom just because genetics had graced him with a gorgeous face?

Mr. Gorgeous stretched out a hand. "Patrick Connor, substitute bus driver and sucker—once, but nevermore."

She couldn't accept his extended hand because she was occupied with the two young combatants. Just as well, because she sure knew where casual little handshakes with the likes of Patrick Connor led.

"Um, hi, I'm Wilson Dana—I mean, I'm Wana—"

Oh crap. Why wouldn't her mouth work for a simple introduction?

He chuckled. "Can I help you? You seem a little swamped."

"Someone locked me out of my clinic—" The morning announcements over the intercom interrupted Dana and she fell silent in response to the loud "Shh, shh" she heard from the students still in line. They weren't shushing her; they were taking the opportunity to shush one another. She used the moment of calm to hand out the next round of medications.

The medicine assembly line went quicker now, and Dana managed to dispense the meds in record time. She double-checked her list, ticked off the last name and breathed a sigh as the door shut.

"That bad?"

"I had no *idea* kids could be so inventive." She leaned against the bulletin board. "I thought that after three weeks I had run the gauntlet of every practical joke a kid could come up with. Maybe I'm not cut out for this job."

She was rewarded with a frown as Patrick surveyed the room as if inspecting it. The frown eased a bit, but concern still tightened his forehead.

"So things aren't settling down for you?" Patrick asked after that moment of inspection. "Your résumé said you could run trauma codes in big-city emergency rooms with one hand tied behind your back. Our superintendent figured that operating a little old school clinic would be a breeze."

The two boys rolled their eyes and snickered.

Dana ignored the noises. The man's familiarity with her set all inner alarms on full alert. Maybe new school nurses were hot gossip in a small town like Logan.

Again, he must have read her expression. "Sorry. When I'm not completely screwing up bus routes and letting kids like these pull each other apart limb by limb, I manage a glass company and am chairman of the board of education. I voted to hire you—on the principal's and superintendent's recommendations, of course."

Dana couldn't subdue the cringe overtaking her. The chaos in her office this morning created exactly the wrong impression she wanted to give the powers that be. She swept the clipboard and other paperwork littering her desk into as tidy a pile as she could.

"No, no, things are settling down nicely. It, uh, just, takes time, I guess."

Patrick skewered her with a stare. She dropped her gaze first to her messy desk, and then swiveled it to the floor, to the copy box of office things she hadn't gotten around to unpacking. Only the loud ticking of the clock and the boys' renewed snickers punctuated the silence. If she could have departicalized and slipped through the molecules of the floor, she would have.

Patrick cleared his throat, obviously preparing for a speech of some sort. To occupy her hands and give her some reason not to meet his eyes, Dana once again shifted the items on her desk from one pile to another.

"Ms. Wilson, could you stop that? It's driving me nuts." His voice was sharp.

She met his gaze, her pulse pounding in her ears, and prepared for the worst.

CHAPTER TWO

PATRICK CONNOR WAS moving his mouth again, but Dana couldn't focus on his words because of the humiliation humming through her veins. Fired. She was going to get fired.

She saw his frustration and knew he realized she wasn't paying the slightest attention. She bit her lip and covered up the action by turning to the two malingerers still lounging in clinic. "Boys, out. You're okay. I'll put your visit slips into your teacher's box, all right?"

They went, grumbling, and Dana recovered some of her composure. She forced a smile at Patrick. "You were saying?"

"Oh. Yeah. Just wanted to be clear that you knew how important getting daily status checks on our asthmatic students was. Nellie prepared weekly reports for me."

Bureaucracy. Red tape had a way of slithering around you until it nearly strangled you. Dana sighed. "Sure. The principal mentioned it to me, though I think daily checks for every asthmatic student we have are a little much. I was hoping we could scale back to perhaps an as-needed basis."

Patrick's eyebrows lowered a fraction of an inch, and his eyes cooled ten degrees. "The board and I would like to be certain our students are okay. It wasn't that much trouble for our other nurse."

Way to go, Wilson. She had wowed him with her disorganization, and now she was questioning his first request. She didn't see the need for the twice daily checks, but she did see the need for food on the table, and that meant keeping her bosses happy. "Of course. You still want morning and afternoon checks, correct? Or can we—"

"Yes. Morning and afternoon checks."

"For all twenty-four asthmatic students?"

"All twenty-four," he confirmed crisply.

"And any new ones that pop up."

"Especially the new ones that pop up." Patrick inclined his head. "Well, I'll let you get back to your day. No doubt you've got a lot to keep you busy." He stared at her littered desktop, then started for the door.

She sighed as she surveyed the mess Patrick had found so offensive. No point kicking herself now over what qualities not to show your new boss. Dana swept the whole mess into the upturned lid of the copy box leaving a clean desk—and a pile of paperwork to get through before the day was done.

He was right. She had a lot to keep her busy.

THE DAY WAS OVER. Finally. The last bell had rung, the buses had pulled out, the halls were eerily quiet—and her copy box was empty. Dana celebrated by stretching her tired body on the exam table in the clinic. The tissue paper crinkled and snapped under her as she wiggled her backside a little lower.

"Comfy yet?" Suze Mitchell, the school vice principal, asked from where she'd collapsed in the plastic chair at Dana's desk. "I come in here to find out whether you survived your day, and you're bent on taking a nap."

"Ha! On this thing? If I were four-foot-nothing, maybe."

"How tall *are* you?" Suze asked. "I'd kill to be anything more than armpit high."

"No, you wouldn't. Try being five-ten for a while."

"You're just five-ten? I would have sworn…"

The petite brunette cast an assessing eye up and down Dana's pretzeled frame.

"I *am* five-ten. Okay…in bare feet…if I scrunch. I'm five-eleven-and-a-half with good posture. Which might explain why I've had such a tough time with relationships. Men get weirded out when the gal is taller than the guy."

Suze chuckled derisively. "Men get weirded out about a lot of things. Commitment. Fidelity. Bank accounts. And even when you find the right man, he still has trouble accepting that he needs to come home every once in a while instead of going hunting and fishing all the time."

"Tell me about it, sister," Dana agreed.

Dana had known from the instant she'd met Suze on her first tour of the school a month ago that the woman would be a keeper friend.

She couldn't explain the connection. It wasn't just the way Suze had jumped in and found her a new place to rent after the house Dana had thought she'd secured had fallen through. It wasn't even that Suze reminded her of her big sister, Tracy, who was older by four years but shorter by at least that many inches. Dana's little sister was smaller than Dana was, too.

No, it had to be the snap of mischief in Suze's dark eyes—a snap you might miss behind the otherwise professional mask. But Dana had spotted it. And that glint had told her she'd found a kindred spirit.

Suze stretched and yawned, her own weariness from the day showing. "So, if I can be nosy, how long have you and your ex been divorced?"

"Three years." Dana stared up at the ceiling and calculated when Marty had presented the papers to her with a flourish. "No, make that nearly four."

"But…" Suze hesitated. The silence hung, awkwardly the ticking of the clock bringing to Dana's mind the morning's earlier awkward silence between her and Patrick.

"But what?"

"Well, it's none of my business, but I assumed your ex was the father of your little girl. And she's, what, three?"

Dana agreed. It was none of Suze's business. She didn't tear her gaze from the ceiling tiles. "He is," she answered cryptically.

"Oh."

Dana could hear the thrum of vacuum cleaners starting up in the halls. Trash cans rattled as they were emptied room by room, the sound nearing the clinic door.

Suze made a show of groaning. When Dana glanced the vice principal's way, Suze wiggled toes she'd liberated from pointy high heels.

"It's getting better, isn't it? You? The job?"

Dana groaned for real. "I'm as tired as if I'd worked a full-moon shift in the E.R. on New Year's Eve. I think I seriously underestimated what a school nurse does. I was darn busy, I didn't even get a chance to pee. And I had at least two kids in here upchucking."

"Pizza," Suze said.

"Pizza?"

"Yeah. They served pizza in the lunchroom today,

and we always have kids upchucking whenever they serve pizza. It's some immutable law. You're lucky it was only two."

"Cooks can't figure out what's going on?"

"Don't ask me."

"And what's with all the neurotic asthma tests?"

Suze cocked her head. "Neurotic asthma tests?"

Dana let her exasperation propel her to a sitting position. "Yeah, the asthma tests I have to do on the kids. Every morning I have to check all twenty-four known asthmatic kids, and every afternoon I have to check them again."

Her thoughts drifted back over her morning conversation with Patrick Connor. His beloved tests added to an already full day and would put her perpetually behind on her daily mountain of paperwork. "Just doing the checks takes a colossal chunk of time out of my day, and that's not counting the tallying up I do on Mr. Gorgeous's Excel spreadsheet."

"Mr. Gorgeous? Who's Mr. Gorgeous?"

Dana's cheeks heated with embarrassment. "Uh, you know. Patrick Connor. The board chairman. The man may be a micromanager and a clean-desk freak, but you have to admit he looks like he's straight out of a cologne ad."

Suze bit her lip. "Yeah. He does that, all right. Most of the women around here tend to agree—at least, until they try to date him for more than two dates running."

"Another commitment-phobe, huh? Figures." Dana recalled the dates her friends had fixed her up with over the years she'd been single. They'd had terrific nights out—until the guys let her know that her friends had neglected to tell them about her daughter. To discover Patrick was the same way didn't surprise her.

Suze's face went blank and she shook her head. "I

really shouldn't comment. But what's this about asthma tests twice a day?"

"I told you. Twenty-four kids twice a day. If they've got asthma on their chart, I've got them on my list."

"I didn't realize—oh, the lunchroom." Comprehension eased the furrow between Suze's eyebrows.

"What does the lunchroom have to do with asthma?"

"We've got documented mold in the lunchroom."

"Huh? That's why I'm checking twenty-four kids?" Dana tried not to gape.

"Yep. About two years ago the roof on the lunchroom building was replaced. The building's got a gable roof now, but it used to have an old flat roof, and it leaked so much the lunchroom ladies had to put five-gallon buckets out on rainy days just to catch the drips. Anyway, when the repair people went in to fix the roof, they found mold. They traced it down inside the concrete blocks and under some of the floor tiles."

"Why is there still mold? Why didn't they get rid of it?"

Suze gave her an amused smile. "The board members sure wished it had been that simple. They figured all they had to do was get in there with a jug of bleach and a scrub brush. But mold, even when it's been killed, can still cause trouble if it's not been properly removed. And it can cost half a million dollars to have professionals do a mold abatement. That's money the school system doesn't have."

"Wait a minute. Are you telling me they left mold—"

"No, well, sort of. They took the do-it-yourself approach. Patrick researched out the yin-yang of how to do it, and one CYA thing he's apparently still doing is these asthma checks."

Dana huffed. "Pardon me, but *he's* not doing the

asthma checks. I am." Now her irritation at having to do twice-daily checks increased. If the school system wasn't going to properly abate the mold, then tracking the school system's most vulnerable population was like holding a hose over a house on fire with no water in the hose.

Suze shrugged. "He's probably afraid of a lawsuit. The whole thing was all hush-hush. The only reason I know anything about it is that I'm vice principal."

Dana's chest tightened. Lawsuits. That was something she knew about only too well. "They haven't told the parents of the kids?" She hopped off the exam table and started pacing the tight confines of the clinic. "I can't believe that! The school has a duty to report—" But she cut off her words. Of course she could believe it.

Suze appeared genuinely miserable. "Hey, I've said way too much."

"No, you've said just enough. I'm going to talk to him."

"Who—Patrick?" Suze blanched. "Listen, you should understand—"

She broke off. Dana peered at her. "Understand what?"

"Could you avoid bringing my name up?"

"They wouldn't fire you for telling me, would they?" Dana gawked at Suze.

"No, no. But Patrick is one stubborn son of a gun, and, well…there's some history between us."

"You dated?"

Suze leaned her head against the wall. "No. Not that kind of history. I'd rather not say, okay? I don't— Patrick's not a bad guy. He just has…issues."

Dana glanced at the clock on the wall. Five minutes

past the time to pick up Kate. Great. "Well, Patrick Connor is about to have a few more issues—because how he's proceeding isn't right."

CHAPTER THREE

ALL PATRICK COULD HEAR in the kitchen was the *thunk* of Melanie's knife on the cutting board, as she whacked up carrots a little harder than necessary, and the tap-tap of Lissa's shoes against the tile floor. The girls had their backs to each other, stiff, unbending.

He'd asked for this. Patrick admonished himself. Self-inflicted agony. He had been the one who said the only thing he wanted for his birthday was a dinner at home with his daughters. Right now, he could have been enjoying a gift card from the home-improvement store.

Patrick sighed and opened the door to the cabinet where the plates were. "Lissa, is that chicken about ready?"

"Uh, yeah. I think so, anyway."

He handed her a plate. "Should I be worried? Should I head for KFC?" he joked.

His effort at levity lifted the corners of Lissa's mouth ever so slightly. For a moment, he was tempted to push the joke. But this was probably the longest sentence his eighteen-year-old daughter had spoken to him in months, and at least she'd looked him in the eye.

I should be thankful she's even agreed to be here. She skipped my birthday last year.

"Dad, salad's ready. Should I toss it with the dressing?"

At Melanie's question, his youngest daughter's tiny smile faded. Patrick's hope for the evening faded right along with it.

He could remember a time when the two girls—no, Mel was a young woman now, and Lissa, for all her immaturity, was nearly one—were not so polarized by sibling rivalry. But then the divorce and everything that had gone on between Jenny and him had destroyed any closeness. The girls had wound up in either their mom's corner—that would be Lissa—or their dad's—that would be Melanie.

Just once he wanted them to forget who had sided with whom and be a family.

Melanie hadn't been happy about Patrick's birthday request, he knew. She'd planned on taking him out to dinner and, he suspected, not asking Lissa to join them. Which was understandable. Lissa had ignored more than one of his birthdays.

Except when she wanted something. So what did she want now?

In a desire to mend fences between him and Melanie, he said, "Your cake looks so good, Mel, that I'm tempted to skip the leafy greens altogether."

She beamed, his approval lessening some of the tension in her still-necked posture. "It was a cinch, Dad. Coconut, your favorite."

"He likes German chocolate, too," Lissa observed as she drained a piece of chicken before dropping it on the plate Patrick had given her.

"No, *Mom* likes German chocolate. Why is it that you can never remember—" But Melanie didn't finish what she was about to say. "The coconut's all right, isn't it?"

"I'm easy to please. Coconut, German chocolate—

doesn't matter to me. But yeah, coconut's my favorite."
Patrick figured that if this strained atmosphere went on
for much longer, his dessert would be Maalox, not cake.

If just he and Lissa had been having this conversation,
he would have come straight out and asked her why she
was even here. What had made her say yes this year when
he'd asked her to spend his birthday with him? Was he
foolish to hope that her coolness toward him was thawing?

He jammed his hand into the silverware drawer,
smothering an oath when the tine of a fork poked him.

Damn Jenny, anyway. She was the one who'd left.
She was the one who'd thought their marriage—their
family, what was left of it, anyway—should be
scrapped. All because some other guy listened to her.
Listened.

Tonight it seemed that he was about to lose Melanie
by trying to salvage what was left of his relationship
with Lissa.

But if he'd learned anything, it was that you were
never guaranteed tomorrow. That and you'd better take
advantage of what you had today. Maybe Lissa felt the
same way. Maybe her first semester at technical college
had rammed home how quickly time flew and how
things could never stay the same.

Lissa, in college now. This was the year Annabelle
should have graduated from high school.

The silverware in his fist slipped out of his grip and
landed with a clatter on the floor. Everybody jumped
at the racket.

For an endless moment, Patrick felt his eyes shift
from Melanie to Lissa and back again.

Then Melanie chuckled. Lissa joined in and Patrick
laughed himself, but out of relief.

"Boy, we're strung tight," Patrick told them.

"Long day." Melanie went back to tossing the salad. "I swear, the phone at my office rang nonstop all afternoon."

"At least you're an accountant and you work in an office. You're not stuck ringing up groceries. Man alive, but I got chewed out for carding somebody who wanted to buy beer," Lissa said. "I wish I could quit. I have to keep this job, though, and my other job to earn the car down payment because *somebody* won't co-sign a loan for me."

Patrick caught Mel's knowing older-sister eye. "Oh, poor baby," she sniped. "Maybe if you had actually done what you were supposed to do and showed a little responsibility, Dad would have a little confidence in you."

"I am responsible! What do you mean?"

"The internship you flaked out on. If you can't get your papers in on time, how can Dad expect you to make a car payment on time?"

"Dad!" Lissa whirled to face Patrick, and jabbed the fork at him. "You told her I missed the deadline?"

Mel didn't wait for Patrick to respond, just jumped in. "Yeah, he did. How else was he supposed to explain his sudden change of heart? You're eighteen, Lissa. Grow up, why don't—"

"Mel, that's enough." Patrick stepped between them. Now he regretted having mentioned Lissa's sad story to her elder sister.

The chicken grease hissed behind them. Lissa broke the stare she had locked on to Mel to attend to it. Her smug look as she turned toward the stove irritated Patrick.

"Lissa, Mel's right about one thing. You need to be more responsible. It's not just the internship paperwork. If you're serious about a job in the nursing profession, you have to manage a lot of deadlines, and that's part of the reason your teachers set them—"

"It's hard, Dad."

Her whine sent his blood pressure up just a tick more. "Yeah, maybe. But when Mel was your age, I never had to worry—"

"Perfect Mel with her perfect husband and her perfect house and her perfect job. Never-screws-up Mel. Never-try-anything-so-you-don't-screw-up Mel." But Lissa's mutter was barely audible. He shook his head toward Mel to stop her retort.

More silence. Patrick grabbed some plates and would have put them down on the small table in the kitchen, but Mel took them from him.

"It's your birthday, Dad," she said. "Even if Luke had to work and we can't all be here, we can eat in the dining room, okay? It's a celebration."

Patrick ignored the derisive sound Lissa made at the mention of Mel's state-trooper husband. "Okay." He headed for the dining room with his stack of plates. Over his shoulder he called, "I can top both of you on the bad day at work. Today was my first and last day as a bus driver—and I had to break up a fight."

"You? Drive a school bus?" Lissa laughed and was leaning back against the cabinet when he returned. "This I gotta hear."

"Why is it that everybody gazes at me like that when I tell them I drove a school bus?" He let mock irritation color his words. "What? I don't appear competent to drive a bus?"

He ventured a glance at Melanie, who was openly curious.

"Go on, Dad. I want to hear."

So he started telling them, spinning the story light and funny and eviscerating from it all details of his momentary heart-stopping look at that little girl. Lissa and Mel were laughing now, a beautiful, beautiful sound.

The doorbell rang, and Melanie wiped her hands on a dish towel, then went headed to answer the front door. "Are you expecting someone? It's not Luke. He won't get home until nearly two in the morning."

"No. But if it's Vann, tell him to come on in. We've got plenty, don't we?"

Lissa lifted her eyebrows in disbelief and held a little tighter to the plate of chicken in her hand. She was the spitting image of Jenny when she did that. "Vann's huge, Dad. Linebacker huge. He could probably clean us out and still ask for seconds."

"According to Vann, it's all muscle, not an ounce of fat." Patrick grinned at Lissa. "But I agree, all that muscle has an appetite."

"Dad?" Melanie's strained voice pierced the house. "Someone's here for you. A Dana Wilson?"

The name jolted Patrick back to this afternoon, back to the school nurse who'd shifted papers from one pile to another and who had admitted maybe she wasn't up to the job. A good thing he hadn't interviewed Dana Wilson for the job. He might have been inclined not to hire her based on how pretty she was. All that blond curly hair and those big brown eyes. And those long legs. Even though her legs had been hidden beneath scrubs, he could tell they were nice.

"Dad?" Melanie sounded even more strained.

"I'm coming. Give me a minute to get there. Why don't you just invite her in."

"She—she—"

Patrick rounded the corner to the living room and

saw Melanie at the door, blocking his view. Mel usually had excellent manners. What was her problem?

He walked up behind Mel. "Dana, hi. Why don't you—"

But Patrick could get no more words out. His throat closed up and he gripped the door. Dana wasn't alone. On her hip was a little girl, blond hair curling softly around her face, thumb in her mouth, sky-blue eyes heavy with drowsiness.

BEWILDERMENT PARALYZED Dana for a long moment. She stood there on Patrick's front porch, switching her gaze from Patrick's befuddled face to his daughter's, and then back again. Both Patrick and his daughter wore expressions of shell shock.

What? Had she grown horns or a second head? Had her hair turned purple?

"I—I thought this was a good time. To talk about the asthma tests," Dana ventured, shifting Kate from one hip to the other. "On the phone you said to come by?"

Patrick frowned. "You called me?"

"No—your daughter here." Dana nodded toward the young woman. "I stopped by your shop, and they said you were on your way home, so I phoned your home and your daughter—"

Melanie folded her arms across her chest. "I haven't spoken to her, Dad. I don't know what she's talking about."

For a second, Dana considered whether she'd dialed the wrong number, but then she recalled the conversation, her careful check to be sure she had the right Patrick Connor. "Well, I certainly talked to someone who said it was okay for me to stop by. Otherwise, why would I be here?"

Patrick pursed his lips. "It's okay. Come in. Forgive my manners." He stepped back, and Dana brushed past him and his daughter.

She knew she wasn't bonkers. She *had* talked to someone who said she was his daughter.

"I'm hungry, Mommy." Kate lifted her head from Dana's shoulder and tugged at her. "Do they got a snack?"

"No snack, sweetie. We'll go home in a few minutes, okay?" Dana patted Kate on the back.

"But you said that a while ago. I'm *hungry*."

"In a minute. Um, I just had some concerns over the asthmatic kids at school." Now that she was here, in the man's living room, Dana had no clue what had possessed her to barge in. This could have waited until Monday.

"Is there a problem?" Patrick seemed to tense from head to toe.

"It's just that—" Shoot. She should have waited. She was totally unprepared, without any sort of speech or script.

"Dad! Dinner's getting cold!"

That sounded more like the person on the phone. Of course. He had *two* daughters.

The owner of the voice arrived into the living room, and Dana saw a girl with long highlighted hair, dressed in a hoodie and skintight jeans——the complete opposite of the dark-haired older daughter in business casual.

"Hi! You must be the nurse," the younger daughter said. "Sorry, Dad. I completely forgot to tell you she phoned. My bad."

Out of the corner of one eye, Dana caught the older daughter's eyes narrowing in disbelief. Ooh, a good case of sibling rivalry here. With two sisters, Dana knew a thing or two about that.

"Uh, Dana, this is my older daughter, Melanie, and I guess you've already talked to Lissa, my younger daughter." Patrick's mouth jerked in an awkward attempt at a smile, but it was considerably dimmer in wattage than the earlier one at Dana's clinic. "Girls, this is Dana Wilson. She's the new nurse at the elementary school."

Melanie's smile was as tight and awkward as Patrick's had been—no small wonder, since she favored him in appearance. Lissa's grin crinkled the girl's big blue eyes and seemed ten degrees warmer than Melanie's.

"Cute little one you've got there," Lissa said. "How old is she?"

"Um, Kate's three. She'll turn four in the summer."

Had Patrick just winced? Was Kate what this cool reception was all about? Figured. He'd been nice enough at the clinic when he hadn't known she had a kid, but the minute he saw a child, he was like every other guy she'd dated since Marty.

Maybe she should save herself a lot of time and trouble and have *single mom* tattooed on her forehead. At least then she wouldn't have to endure a guy's hot and cold reactions.

"Mommy," Kate whimpered. "I'm hungry. Please?"

"Hey, why don't you guys eat with us. Does fried chicken, tossed salad, butter beans, cream corn and rolls sound good?" Lissa rubbed her hands together. "Dad was just saying we had plenty."

CHAPTER FOUR

FOR THE LIFE OF HER, Dana couldn't figure out how she came to be sitting at a dinner table with Patrick and his two daughters, one of whom was staring daggers at her.

She cast a glance at Kate, who was eating up Lissa's attention. Usually, Kate was shy and hesitant with strangers, but not with Lissa. Lissa had her in giggles within seconds—and the fried chicken on Kate's plate had sealed the deal.

At least one daughter was kid friendly.

The jury was still out on Patrick. After Lissa's off-the-cuff invitation, he'd heartily agreed. Yes, absolutely, she must join them.

She'd overheard Melanie hiss, "But, Dad! This is your birthday supper!" and Dana had tried to leave then. Patrick wouldn't hear of it.

"No, no, it's fine. This is no big deal. Only supper and a cake. You like cake, don't you? Melanie makes a mean coconut cake."

The tension at the table dissipated as Patrick shook out his napkin and passed around the platter of chicken. "I was just telling the girls about my two wannabe professional wrestlers this morning. How'd they do, anyway?"

"I didn't hear a peep out of them all day long, so I guess they must have survived." Dana took a piece of chicken and handed the platter to Melanie. "This looks great!"

"Lissa fried it. I hope you can eat it." If Dana was reading Melanie's underlying sentiment correctly, the truer words would have been, *I hope you get an ulcer*.

But Dana just ignored Melanie's remark and switched her praise to Lissa. "You're a better cook than me. I never fool with frying chicken."

"My mom is the best cook, and we do a lot of cooking together," Lissa told her.

Dana recalled Suze's allusions to Patrick's divorced status and wasn't sure what to say. She mumbled, "That's nice."

On the heels of that awkward moment came another when Lissa skewered her with blue eyes alight with curiosity. "So are you and Dad seeing each other?"

Dana dropped the piece of chicken she held and Patrick choked on butter beans he was eating.

"Uh, no, actually, we're not. I met your father for the first time today."

"Oh. That's nice." Lissa beamed. "I just figured, you know, you calling, looking for him on his birthday—you know."

Dana picked up the drumstick with numb fingers. "No. No. Remember? I mentioned on the phone that this had to do with the clinic at school."

Melanie seemed to relax a bit then. Dana wondered if perhaps Melanie's earlier reaction derived from the same wrong conclusion Lissa had jumped to.

"I like this corn, Mommy! Why doesn't our corn taste this way?"

"I don't know, sweetheart." Dana felt her cheeks heat up. She chuckled and said to Patrick and his daughters, "I did say I wasn't much of a cook."

"Kate, it's probably because we grew this corn ourselves," Patrick offered.

Kate frowned. "My mommy buys corn in cans."

Lissa laughed; Melanie managed a subdued chuckle and Dana cringed. At least Kate's confession indicated Dana attempted to cook. If Kate kept going, she'd probably tell them just how many trips to the McDonald's drive-thru she and Kate made.

Patrick nodded to Kate. "Well, yeah, I guess she does. That's what a lot of people do. But we grow it." He turned to Dana. "My older sister and her husband live out in the country and we grow a big garden together."

"That's very nice."

"You have brothers or sisters?"

"Two sisters. I'm in the middle."

"Are they as tall as you?" Lissa asked.

Melanie again shot daggers, but now at her little sister. Dana smothered a laugh, remembering how many times her older sister had tried—and failed—to keep her straight.

"Uh, no. My older sister is a little above average height, and my younger one is on the petite side. She likes to say she's vertically challenged."

"Oh, that's like my aunt. She always says—"

"Lissa, can you get us some more ice?" Melanie broke in. "Dana's glass needs refreshing."

The interruption caught Dana by surprise. What had that been all about?

But Lissa shoved back her chair with an under-the-breath mumble about bossy older sisters and Patrick interjected a question about where Dana had found a place to live, and she pushed aside her curiosity and answered his question.

The rest of the meal went smoothly enough. Civil, polite on Melanie and Patrick's part; effusively warm on Lissa's part. Dana had to admit that Lissa was a sheer wonder with Kate, and acknowledged it was great to have a meal where she had some help retrieving dropped spoons and napkins, cutting up the food into bite-size pieces, making a quick save of a toppling glass. Lissa was a natural.

When Dana remarked on it, Lissa told her, "I like kids, especially this age. I babysit a lot during the summer, and I have a little brother. He's six now, but you know, my mom needed help. I'm going to school to be a nurse, and I hope I get to work with pedes."

"Oh. I see. You'll be good at it."

Lissa beamed. "If you ever need somebody to watch Kate, I'll be glad to do it. I've got excellent references."

Dana grinned. Had Lissa's motivation simply been to drum up business? If so, the gambit had been an effective one. "I don't get out much, but I'll keep you in mind."

Not until the lighting of Patrick's birthday cake did Dana find herself feeling awkward and in the way. Melanie brought in the cake, aglow with too many candles for Dana to count, though she did try to figure out Patrick's age.

Then Lissa started singing "Happy Birthday" in a clear, beautiful alto and urged everyone to join in. Kate sang along without any prompting, but Dana hesitated. She felt shy and uncertain about singing "Happy Birthday" to a man she'd only just met.

Her eyes searched out cues from Melanie and Lissa and then finally Patrick. His gaze wasn't on his daughters or the cake. It was locked on Kate as she lisped out the song. His jaw was set, his lips compressed.

The Patrick Connor she'd seen earlier in the day had

vanished. Whatever interest he'd shown in Dana had vanished, as well.

She'd encountered that reaction too many times not to know it for what it was. The first time was the day she'd told Marty she was pregnant. His face had gone from happy anticipation at the prospect of big news to complete and utter gray-white shock when he learned what that news was.

Marty had tried to muscle his way through the moment, but he'd looked a lot the way Patrick Connor did now. No doubt about it. Patrick—as did most of the men who followed in Marty's footsteps—had a problem with kids.

EVERY LITTLE OFF-KEY note that Kate Wilson sang knifed Patrick.

She's not Annabelle. She doesn't even resemble Annabelle.

That he'd even been able to speak when he'd seen the child on Dana's hip had been a sheer miracle. If he'd just had some sort of warning…

Dana had to think he was a loon. He couldn't believe it when he'd impulsively agreed with Lissa that she and Kate should join them for supper. Part of him had been eager to seize on anything that would encourage any rapprochement with Lissa.

And the other part?

Sheer insanity.

After supper, Patrick followed the girls into the kitchen with his plate, while Dana stayed at the table, cleaning up after Kate. Kate's giggle floated after him.

God, so much time had passed since a baby had been in the house. He'd forgotten what wonderful music their giggles made.

Patrick found Melanie and Lissa in an argument, carried on in low hisses at the sink.

"Like you *really* forgot to tell Dad some woman had called. And to invite her here when you were aware it was Dad's birthday."

"She's *nice,* Melanie! What's the problem?"

"The problem is you're up to something, and I know it, Lissa, so don't—"

"You never believe me, so why should I bother saying anything at all? I forgot. Take it or leave it."

"Girls." At Patrick's voice, they jumped guiltily. "We have a guest. One whom one of you invited."

"Not me. Dad, you're not going to start dating her, are you? I mean, she has a…" Melanie bit her lip.

Lissa put her hands on her hips. "Say it. You can say it. The world won't end if you do. She has a child."

The corners of Melanie's mouth turned down. "That's rather obvious. Did you know that when you invited her to party-crash?"

"No. But I sure would have invited her if I had. Because I just love to watch you wig out. You still haven't gotten over Mom having Christopher and he's six now," Lissa said.

Melanie blanched at Lissa's second mention of their stepbrother. "That's—I don't want to talk about it."

"Girls. Enough." Patrick glanced behind him to make sure Dana and Kate hadn't left the dining room, then spoke in a low voice. "Let's not fight on my birthday, especially when we have a guest. And Melanie, I've barely met the woman. Of course I'm not dating her. If I were, though, it's my business."

Melanie rolled her eyes at Lissa's triumphant little "Yes!" complete with dragged-down fist gesture.

"You think you want this, but you don't have a clue,

do you? You don't care about anybody but you. You've completely ruined Dad's birthday, all because you're a drama queen," Melanie said.

After Patrick shot her a warning look, she waved away whatever else she was going to add. "Okay, okay. I won't say any more. You deal with Lissa."

"Later. And that's a promise, Lissa." He set his plate on the countertop. "Right now, I'm going to attempt to be a good host."

When he returned to the dining room, Kate was cleaned up and Dana was gathering her things. "I am so sorry to have interrupted this night. I should have thought things through and waited until Monday."

Patrick curled his fingers around the woodwork on the dining room chair. "You said something about the asthma tests. So what's on your mind?"

"I should go. It'll keep—I am so sorry."

"No problem. We enjoyed having you."

Dana didn't seem at all convinced by his words, and he had to admit they sounded insincere. He tried again. "Lissa enjoyed having you guys here tonight, and I'm grateful for that. She's at a…well, a difficult age."

Dana's smile didn't quite reach her eyes. "Yes. I'm glad to be of service. Now, I'll get out of your hair and be on my way, and perhaps we can talk about this on Monday."

"Talk about what? You never did tell me precisely," he pointed out.

She stopped in the middle of stuffing some child gear into her oversize purse. "The asthmatic kids. The mold. Why didn't you tell me about the mold?"

Her accusatory question caught him as off guard as Kate's rendition of "Happy Birthday" had. Patrick rubbed at his eyes, struggling to figure out how to respond.

"I thought Vann—" No. That was a lie. He knew Vann well enough to realize that Vann wouldn't have immediately offered up that information without asking him first.

"Yes?" Now her tone had an edge to it, cool and crisp.

"We should have. I should have. I'm sorry."

"Is this a cover-up? Am I part of a bean-counting process?"

"No! No, of course not. We're just trying to do due diligence—"

"If you're trying to do due diligence, how about getting in professionals to eliminate the mold? Instead of tackling a job that's beyond an amateur's scope," she added equably.

"Can I take you up on that offer to talk about this Monday? Because I am not up to it tonight. Consider it a birthday gift." Patrick added that last bit as a joke, but it fell flat.

Dana scooped up Kate and slung the strap of her bag over her shoulder. "Fine. You know where to find me. I'll be the one spending two hours every morning and two hours every afternoon doing useless asthma tests that don't really tell you much of anything."

She marched to the front door. Patrick followed her out, down the steps and to her car.

"Listen, if you want, we can talk about this now."

"No, you're right. I need a weekend to cool off."

He took a step back. "Sure. Then okay. I'll talk to you Monday. It was…nice having you here tonight. You and, um, Kate."

He hadn't intended to say those last words and he wasn't sure where the sentiment had come from.

The words had the effect of arresting Dana as she

put a sleepy Kate into her car seat. "If you mean that, then I'm glad."

She slid behind the wheel of her car, gave him a brief, inscrutable smile and backed around.

Leaving Patrick standing there, wondering, had he meant what he'd said? And what if he had?

CHAPTER FIVE

THE FIRST THINGS that greeted Patrick when he stopped in Dana's clinic on Monday morning were a Christmas wreath on the door and a picture of Kate and Dana, prominently displayed on Dana's spick-and-span desk. He lifted his gaze from the photo to see Dana's cool expression. Her message could not be clearer had she shouted it from the rooftops: *I'm a package deal.*

Or maybe that was just him, not her at all. Maybe she didn't even think about him as date material and she was simply pissed about the mold.

Dana didn't spare him much of a glance as she finished up with a freckle-faced kid. She jotted down some numbers in a file and tapped on her keyboard to enter the same numbers into an Excel spreadsheet—his spreadsheet, he realized, the one that he'd devised to track all the asthmatic kids. "Okay, you're good."

"So why do I have to stop by here every day?" the boy asked. "My asthma's not bad. I haven't had an attack in, like, ages. This is embarrassing!"

"Uh…" Dana shrugged. "Beats me, kiddo. I just do what they tell me to do. It's probably for tracking purposes."

"Oh. Okay. But can you tell 'em that the other kids tease me? And I promise I'll come if I need to, but I've got my inhaler."

Dana fixed an eye on Patrick but continued to address the boy. "Don't worry. I'll tell 'em."

The boy left. Once the door shut behind him, the silence in the room stretched to the breaking point. Patrick cleared his throat and leaned against the clinic counter.

"So. You wanted to talk. I'm here."

"Thank you. I know you said the other nurse did this, but already I'm getting huge complaints from the teachers and the parents about pulling their kids out of class. The asthma kids."

Patrick considered. He'd never heard complaints about how Nellie had done it. Maybe Dana was doing it in a different way. "It won't kill them. It takes, what, five minutes per kid?"

"Right." Dana reclined in her desk chair, crossing those fabulous legs of hers. She folded her arms over her chest. "That's five minutes for me to do a peak-flow meter reading and to listen to their chest and to note the results. But it's five minutes here and five minutes back to class. That's fifteen minutes. Multiply that by two times a day, and that means that each of those students is losing thirty minutes of instruction a day."

Patrick found himself nodding and froze. Was he agreeing with her just because she was so damn pretty? He had to remember that he'd had good reasons for asking for this, reasons that didn't disappear because some kid felt embarrassed by the attention or an attractive nurse was questioning the task. "Well, can't you do it at recess? Or during rotation?"

"You want parents to really get riled? Take away a kid's recess. Besides, you requested this twice a day, remember? That means morning and afternoon."

"We have to be certain the students aren't—"

"You mean, you have to be certain the school isn't making them any sicker," she snapped. "Isn't that the bottom line? Liability?"

Patrick shifted on his feet. On the bulletin board, the middle finger on the laminated hand still stuck up in an offensive gesture. It annoyed him, so he scooped up Dana's stapler and crossed the room to the board. He rammed the stapler harder than he should have, fixing the fingers.

As he pounded the last staple in, the door flew open, sending the Christmas wreath askew. The principal stuck his head in, gasping for breath. Harrison's eyes were wide, his tie flying. "Ms. Wilson! Ms. Wilson, come quick!"

"What's happened?" Dana was on her feet, pushing past Patrick.

"One of our second-graders…on the monkey bars."

Patrick dropped the stapler and pursued the two adults down the hall, out the back doors of the school. A kid's high-pitched screams punctuated the dreary gray morning of early December.

Dana's long legs had overtaken Harrison's short, stubby ones. Harrison's potbelly slowed him down more, and now Patrick pulled up even with the struggling principal.

"What happened? Did someone fall? Do we need to call an ambulance?"

But Harrison couldn't get the words out. He bent over, palms on his knees, and sucked wind. "She's…on…" Unable to say more, he pointed a finger toward the monkey bars.

High up, on the top rung of the ancient metal jungle gym that Patrick remembered the PTO putting in when Lissa and Mel were in elementary school, sat the source of the screams.

Patrick drew to a standstill beside Dana at the foot of the monkey bars, joining a crowd of small-fry on-lookers. The girl had one hand on a rung, and was using the other hand to shoo away the angry buzzing yellow jackets swarming around her head.

"Honey, honey!" Dana called. "Are you stung?"

"Get 'em away! Get 'em away!" the girl shrieked.

"Are you stung?" Dana asked again.

But the girl couldn't answer. Patrick heard Dana sigh. Without warning, Dana yanked a rung and began the climb to join the girl, whose head poked through the cloud of buzzing insects.

"Okay, sweetheart, no—no, don't swat at them. That will just make them angrier," Dana cautioned. She took the little girl by the shoulder. "Are you stung? Let's get you down."

"I—I can't." Tears streaked down the girl's face. "I'm scared. What if they sting me?"

"Uh, they will if we stay up here much longer. C'mon. What's your name?"

"Jakayla."

"Jakayla. That's a pretty name. C'mon. I'll bet you've climbed down lots of—"

The girl shook her head violently and tightened her grip on the bar. The movement kick-started the yellow jackets into even more activity.

"Okay, okay." As she pondered the problem of how to get the girl down, Dana seemed mindless of the two yellow jackets that had landed on her scrubs.

Patrick swung up. "Jakayla?" He was now face-to-face with her. "I'll help. Ms. Wilson and I've got you. You just close your eyes."

"But then I can't see 'em!" she protested.

That's the point. "Trust us. We won't let you get

stung, but we do need to get you down. I'm holding you." He wrapped his hands around the girl's chunky waist. "Close your eyes."

Jakayla sucked in a labored breath and squeezed shut terrified eyes. Patrick tugged, but the girl's grip hadn't lessened. Dana made a noise that sounded suspiciously like a smothered chuckle and began peeling the girl's sweaty fingers, one by one, off the metal bar.

Patrick took a step down, and with one hand still on Jakayla's waist, he used the other to steady himself. But he'd miscalculated and not looked where he'd placed his hand. The sting of a yellow jacket needled through his palm.

Dana could tell he was attempting to stifle the groan the sting evoked. "Patrick?"

He shook his head, unwilling to alarm Jakayla any more than she already was. Tears still oozed from the girl's eyes. At least the shrieking had stopped, though.

Together, he with his sore hand and Dana with her good hands lowered the little girl to the ground. Then, Dana at once began inspecting Jakayla for stings. Finding none, she gave the girl a quick hug and turned her attention to Patrick.

"Let's have a look at that palm."

Now Jakayla barreled from between them to her teacher, who waited with comforting arms.

Patrick refused. "It's okay."

"It's swelling. You're not allergic, are you?"

He inspected his hand, which had indeed swollen to a princely size. "Well, this will be a pain."

"I need to check if the stinger's still in there."

"Wait. Harrison?" Patrick found the principal among the crowd of onlookers. "Do you have any wasp or hornet spray? There must be a nest in one of those pipes."

Harrison shuddered. "Oh, dear, yes, I expect that is what happened. I'll get the janitor to spray it."

"Got any of that foam aerosol insulation? The stuff to fill cracks?"

"I'm not sure." Harrison seemed befuddled by the question and amazed that Patrick expected him to instantly recall what maintenance supplies the school had on hand.

"If you do, we should spray those pipes." He gestured at the open ends. "That way, no yellow jackets or wasps can nest there."

Patrick's hand throbbed now. He shook it. Dana jerked her head toward the school door. "C'mon. Ice and a dose of Benadryl—how about it?"

This time he didn't have to be asked twice. He followed her in.

"Thanks," Dana told him.

"For what?"

"Helping. You saw how tight a grip that girl had. She wasn't going anywhere. I would have had to hit her over the head to get her down without your help."

"Natch. Well, except for the hand." He stared at the puffy hand in disgust. "Why hasn't Harrison inspected that playground equipment? We have kids with severe allergies to bee stings."

They were back at her clinic. She pulled out the chair and pushed him lightly into it. With nimble fingers, she ran a hands-free magnifying glass over his palm and surveyed the damage. "Yep. A stinger, still in there." One tug with some tweezers, and she was done.

She wheeled her stool around to the fridge and drew out an ice pack. "That will help the swelling. If we could have gotten bleach on the sting before it began swelling, you wouldn't have had such a reaction."

"Bleach?"

"Yeah. Bleach. No matter. Open up." Dana flicked on a penlight and wielded a tongue depressor.

"Huh?"

"Your airway. I need to be sure it's not swelling."

"I'm not—oh, okay." He complied, feeling silly. The click off of the penlight told him she was satisfied with her exam.

"A dose of Benadryl and you're good." Dana presented him with several petal-pink tablets. "Sorry. Only have the chewables. They're berry-flavored, but they'll do the job."

He chomped on the sugary-tart tablets. "You're terrific at this."

Dana laughed and began cleaning up. "I'd hope so. Why? You have doubts about my ability?"

"No, but you said it yourself. That first day we met."

Her face colored. "Great way to inspire confidence in your boss, huh?"

"It's okay. From what I saw out in the school yard there, I have no doubts we hired the right nurse. Nell wouldn't have climbed up there after a kid, and if we'd waited on Harrison, Miss Jakayla would have been stung about a dozen times by now."

"All part of a day's work." Dana rose and crossed to the sink, where she began scrubbing the tweezers.

"Well, it shouldn't have been. Harrison has to keep a closer eye on the playground equipment. If that child had fallen and broken an arm or her leg or—God forbid—her neck, her parents could have sent our liability rates through the roof."

Dana's back stiffened. "Ah. More lawsuit paranoia. And I thought you actually cared about Jakayla. But it's like the mold, isn't it? Some parent might sue."

Patrick rose to his feet, his hand hurting like crazy. "You make it sound as though we're heartless. But we've done all we can, I assure you. Once we found the mold—and God knows how long it had been there undetected—we moved rapidly to get it abated. We called in crews to do the work—hell, I got in there myself. I wanted the job done this summer, before school opened."

"But you're still worried. Or else you wouldn't be insisting on this neurotic testing slate." She shook water droplets off the tweezers and faced him. "Your whole testing regime is positively phobic, especially when these tests, without a good baseline from the children's doctors, are practically useless."

"Of course I'm still worried. Only an idiot wouldn't be. I had three choices, Dana. I could hire a professional mold abatement company. Now, that's a racket—the cheapest one wanted a half-million dollars! Or I could put in mobile units—figure two hundred grand there. Or we could do the best job we could ourselves for about sixty thousand dollars." He blew out a long breath. "We're a small, rural school in one of the poorest counties in Georgia. So I didn't have much choice at all."

"Why not go with the mobile units?" she asked. "Surely that would have been the better solution."

"No. Because for one thing, we'd have to pay big bucks for a lunchroom-size unit, or use several smaller ones, instead. Plus, from a health standpoint, a lot of area schools have had health complaints from students when they do put in mobile units for classrooms, and we get severe weather here in the spring. We're at risk for tornadoes off any hurricane that might hit. What's more, I can put that spare hundred forty thousand in the bank toward a brand-spanking new school, which would solve all our problems."

Had anything he'd said sunk in? He couldn't tell. Dana twirled the tweezers in her fingers absently.

"Funds for school facilities are limited," he continued

"Why not build the school now? This building is old. Sure, it's been renovated, but—"

Patrick scoffed and pushed the chair back into its place. "Because I had no other choice. We just don't have the money, not without going to the taxpayers with a hefty tax increase."

"Do it. Ask them. I'll back you up. I'll explain how the mold endangers—"

"No! I do not want to start a panic. You have no idea what you're suggesting. Talking about this would be like crying 'Fire!' in a crowded theater."

He could deduce from her stubborn expression that she just didn't get this at all. "Look," he said, modulating his tone. "If a parent asks, give them the truth. I'm not saying cover anything up. But I'm *suggesting* that we simply don't volunteer the information."

"Uh-huh." Her voice was flat, the tweezers in her fingers still.

"Let's hear it from your point of view. What good would it do to sound the alert? Since we have no funds to do anything else beyond what we've done." He splayed his hands. "I'm open to suggestion."

Now the tweezers beat out a rhythm against the palm of Dana's hand. "An informed parent is always the one less likely to sue," she noted. "And suing is what you're actually worried about."

"No, it's not. At least, not the only thing. And I'm insulted that you think that about me. I have two daughters myself." Patrick found the clinic too small to get a decent pacing going, but it wasn't for lack of trying. "You met them. You believe I don't understand the concerns of the average parent?"

"Then think like one!" She pushed from the counter and stood toe to toe in front of him, blocking his pacing. "Remember, these parents don't have all the information they need to decide whether their kids should attend this school."

She was so close to him that he caught her scent. Some sort of fruit? Peaches. It *was* peaches. He shut his eyes and swallowed, trying hard to focus on her words. If he could just focus on the mold issue and not on what scent she wore, he could defend his reasoning.

"That might make a difference in Savannah, where there's more than one elementary school, but not here," Patrick stated. "We're the only game in town, and most of our parents can't afford transportation and tuition costs to another school."

"Shouldn't this school system be offering to help with that?"

The hairs on the back of his neck prickled and his hand throbbed even more. How could she look so sweet and say things that scared the crap out of him?

"We're fully prepared to offer..." Damn. That peaches smell again. He blinked and stepped back. Better. Much better. He could think now. "If you feel we should offer the asthmatic children that option—"

Demon woman that she was, she stepped closer to him again, intent on driving home her point—or driving him insane. "Relax. I was just wondering if that responsibility had completely escaped you." She appeared yet more disappointed in him than earlier, if that was possible, and that it bothered him confused him even more. "In the long run, it would be cheaper to buy mobile units. At least you'd get them paid for. Transportation and tuition costs are never ending."

He made an effort to move back to escape her nearness, but the edge of the exam table jabbed into his left kidney.

"You know, you're talking to the wrong person. I'm only one vote, and most of the time I'm just a tie-breaker. If you're so passionate about this—" Suddenly the word *passionate* and the smell of peaches together in Patrick's overheated brain induced a three-second fantasy about whether she'd taste as good as she smelled.

She didn't back down. "I *am* passionate about this. If you're just the tiebreaker, I need to be talking to the board. When's the next meeting? I want to be there."

Man, had he ever muffed this. Either way, whether he said yes or no, he was a big-time loser in this proposition.

"It's tomorrow night. We meet once a month. I'll add you to the agenda." With that, he fled the hypnotic effect of the smell of peaches.

Tuesday night found Dana a bundle of nerves. She was never good at public speaking, not since fourth grade when she'd barfed in front of her social studies class during a report on the state of Maine.

Dana had to be honest with herself: she would have run out the door, back home, where Lissa was watching Kate, if Patrick hadn't placed a hand on her elbow the moment she walked in the door.

He steered her through the lobby, past the Christmas tree and holly the staff had put up, into the superintendent's office, where Vann Hobbes was gathering up papers in preparation for the meeting. To Dana, he didn't look like her idea of a superintendent. Aside from his football-player appearance, he seemed far too young to shoulder the responsibility of the whole school system.

"Hey, Vann," Patrick greeted him. "Anything I should know?"

"Guess not— Oh. That guy from the paper is here. Hope he can manage to get the quotes right this time. Last time he had things so screwed up...." Vann shook his head and gave the papers in his hands a final tap.

Patrick cursed. "Why couldn't the little pipsqueak have had something better to do tonight? Just my luck."

Dana saw the mild reproach Hobbes shot toward Patrick. The superintendent swiveled his gaze to her. "Ms. Wilson, you look a little green around the gills. We won't bite. Promise."

"I, uh, I've never been good at speaking in front of crowds," Dana admitted.

"Except for the guy from the paper, it's only me and Patrick and four other board members. Patrick said you had some concerns about the mold and the way we're tracking the students."

Dana swallowed. "I do. I still don't know what possessed me to say I wanted to do this."

Hobbes grinned. "You'd better watch this fellow. He'll have you saying yes to a lot of things you hadn't planned on. He's got his finger on everybody's 'Yes, of course' button. I've known him all my life and I still haven't figured out how does it."

He certainly found my *"yes, of course" button*. Dana pushed away the memory of standing close enough to kiss Patrick, of actually hoping that he might. Which was stupid, stupid, stupid. She'd insulted his whole handling of this issue. Why on earth would he want to kiss her?

But he'd offered her this opportunity to speak out, so maybe he was wishing that if the board heard the seriousness of the situation from someone else, maybe something more could be done. She'd felt vindicated at first by his concession. Then, when the reality of having to speak in public hit her, she'd gotten scared to bits.

Now, in the boardroom, she felt the curious eyes of the other board members on her. From their name-plates, she put the names Mitchell Curtis and Johnny Evans to the men to the right of Patrick, and Gabriella Jones to the lone woman on the board, who sat on Patrick's left with another man, Joel Gibson.

At least Gabriella Jones accorded her a welcoming smile. Dana smiled back, then glanced around the boardroom, which was big enough for the board table and a few chairs for spectators.

Patrick busied himself with the stack of papers in front of him. Even the faded chambray shirt he wore couldn't detract from his good looks. Dana tried not to think about how disappointed she'd been at his reaction to Kate, or how he'd protested at her asking for Lissa's number to babysit Kate tonight.

"I'm not certain she doesn't have plans. She may have a test or something," he'd said. But finally he'd relented and given her Lissa's number.

Lissa had responded enthusiastically, "Of course I'll babysit Kate." And she had shown up a blessed twenty minutes early, to boot. Dana had had time to change her mind twice about what outfit to wear.

Not that she was attempting to impress Patrick. She knew better. A guy was not going to be interested in any woman with a child, and she would be crazy to think otherwise.

Patrick must have sensed her peering at him, because he glanced up from the papers in his hands and caught her eye. He hesitated, then treated her to a nod and a smile. She smiled back and forced herself to look away.

The young string bean of a fellow slouched in a chair two seats down from Dana must be the reporter from the local paper. He was doodling along the top of the notepad he had flipped open. Her stomach went all queasy again at the thought that whatever she said might well be in this week's paper.

Was Patrick right? Could she incite a panic? Or had he just been calling her bluff by agreeing for her to be here?

Dana struggled to cover her nerves by reviewing the notes she'd jotted down on index cards. She peeked at her watch: straight up seven o'clock.

As if on cue, Vann Hobbes rose to his feet and faced the flag in the corner of the room, his hand going for his chest. He cleared his throat and said, "Let's stand for the Pledge of Allegiance."

For the first part of the board meeting, Dana sat through mind-numbing talk of budgets and field trip approvals and the other administrative items on the agenda. She noticed the reporter didn't bother to disguise his boredom. His notepad appeared littered with more lightning bolts and thunderclouds than notes, and the notes he did have were brief: field trip, operating fund, bus maintenance.

How did Patrick manage to endure this month after month? It would drive Dana nuts.

But the reporter perked up when the superintendent switched gears to the mold issue at the school. At the mere mention of the word *mold,* the kid leaned over his pad, his pen poised.

His eagerness made Dana choose her words with extra care. "I want to thank you for allowing me the chance to speak to you," she said, reading off her first index card. She glanced up and saw Patrick staring at her. Her heart skipped a beat. Was this some sort of test?

"Thank *you* for giving up your evening," Patrick told her. The comment, and the unexpected kindness in his voice, was enough to settle some of her nerves. "I understand you have some concerns about how we've abated the mold we discovered during repairs of the lunchroom."

"Yes. I know you did the best that you could with the funds available at the time—" Dana was gratified by the way the Patrick's clenched fist relaxed at her words "—but I'm afraid that the intensive testing you're asking me to do is not serving its purpose. Without a baseline measure, checking the peak-flow meter readings of asthmatic children is not…well, it's meaningless."

Gabriella Jones sat forward intently. "So how do we ensure that these kids are okay and that any residual levels of mold are not affecting them?"

"Um, you can't. Not really. Unless we can discern trends over the entire testing population, daily tests aren't any better than weekly tests." Dana elaborated on the amount of instruction time the children were missing, and she was pleased to note heads nodding in agreement.

Patrick, though, looked grim. He tapped a pencil on the notepad in front of him. "So what are you suggesting?"

"Well, the real solution, the ultimate solution, would be to take the mold out of the equation altogether. I don't believe that a do-it-yourself project would be effective enough to eradicate all the mold. Plus, you've got lunchroom workers and faculty who are similarly exposed. Granted, the faculty and staff are like the kids, minimally exposed because they're in the lunchroom for brief periods of time. But the lunchroom workers spend their working days in there. This could be…" She glanced at the string-bean reporter, who was madly scribbling all this down. "They have reason to go to OSHA."

At the mention of the Occupational Safety and Health Administration, the point on the pencil in Patrick's hand snapped. His jaw worked, and she could tell that he was holding back what he wanted to say.

"We've informed the lunchroom workers and the janitorial staff, and we've had no Workers' Comp complaints," Patrick replied evenly.

"Yet," Dana muttered.

"I beg your pardon?"

"I said yet. You haven't had complaints yet. Why not beg or borrow the money to put in mobile units? If this can be done for the troops in Iraq, surely someone can make a school-cafeteria-size mobile unit. Later on, you can sell it."

Her suggestion was met with silence interrupted only by the thrum of the air-conditioning unit. The board members exchanged glances but waited for Patrick to lead the discussion.

"I agree that we should be looking out for the students' welfare." Patrick's comment was apparently the signal for the other board members to relax. They settled into their chairs, only to spring back to alert with his next words. "Let's face it. Our elementary school is over fifty years old. We cannot keep patching the old girl together with staples and bailing wire."

Evans and Curtis rolled their eyes. "Not the school bond issue again, Patrick," Curtis said. "Voters have been pretty clear they don't want tax increases. We've got the millage rate sky-high as it is."

"*Voters* haven't had a chance to voice an opinion because the issue hasn't even gotten on a ballot due to the board's repeated refusal even to entertain a referendum on the matter," Patrick said sharply.

"And why," Evans inquired, "do we need to go to the trouble and expense of a referendum when we know how it'll turn out?"

"Because, despite what you two may think, the residents of this county—the parents of the children at this school—deserve the chance to decide for themselves. An up or down vote—that's all I'm asking for."

"Yeah, well, you can keep on asking." Evans slammed down his pencil. "And you can keep on asking about mold abatement, too, as far as I'm concerned. I was elected to be a responsible steward of taxpayer dollars, and I just can't comprehend why we should shell out this much money to prevent sniffly noses, no matter how many pretty nurses you parade in front of us. I understand what you're trying to do here—you're trying to paint us in a corner. Why spend two hundred thousand on a bunch of glorified double-wide trailers when we can spend a million and have a new school? Well, we can just make do. We spent tens of thousands of dollars to get rid of that mold, and you're the one who's worried it's not gone. And there she is, your own expert, telling us that we don't even have to go to the trouble of testing these kids every day."

The other two men on the board nodded. Even Gabriella Jones appeared conflicted.

"No. That's not what I meant," Dana protested.

But Patrick didn't give her a chance to finish. "Look, I agree. The taxpayers have made it abundantly clear that they don't want taxes to go up. And I don't know where we'd get the money to buy the mobile units Ms.

Wilson is suggesting. We certainly don't have the re-
sources that the Department of Defense has. But I'm
open to suggestion—I am *always* open to suggestion.
And she's right. Removing the mold from the equation
with new facilities is the best course of action. Can we
afford that? We couldn't last spring, and we can't now.
Not unless the taxpayers see the value in a new school."

What a waste of her time! Had he brought her here
simply to get his point across? Was she just some sort
of political tool? Incensed, Dana snatched up her purse.
"Well, I've shared my concerns, and I can see just how
open to suggestion you are. If you gentlemen—and
Ms. Jones—will excuse me, I have the rest of that
evening Mr. Connor mentioned a while ago."

She didn't wait for them to say she could go. Instead,
she dashed down the hall and out into the night. In her
car, she put her head down on the steering wheel, her
heart thumping. Tears of frustration and disappointment—in Patrick, in herself for even thinking that
Patrick's offer actually meant something—pricked her
eyes.

You couldn't trust men. They would say anything
and then do what they pleased. Hadn't she learned
anything from Marty?

CHAPTER SIX

A RAP ON THE WINDOW sent Dana's already racing pulse into overdrive. She jerked up to find Patrick peering into the car with a frown.

She inched the window down enough to snap, "Don't you have a meeting to finish?"

The frown on Patrick's face dissolved into surprise. He opened his mouth to say something. Offer an excuse, maybe? She didn't know, didn't care. But whatever it was, he bit it back and looked away for a moment. Then he faced her once again.

"I'm sorry." He jammed his fingers into the pockets of his jeans—jeans whose sleek fit Dana wished she hadn't noticed. "I realize you were hoping for more."

"I was hoping—oh, never mind."

"This is ridiculous. Can you get out of the car? I only have a minute or so, and bending down this way is giving me a crick in my neck."

"Good, because you've been a total pain in my neck the whole evening. Why did you completely waste my time?" She clenched the steering wheel.

"Come on. Two minutes. That's all I have and all I'm asking for. You're tall. You know how uncomfortable it is to scrunch down." Patrick cocked his head. "Please?"

She considered his request. What could he say in two

minutes that would change anything? Still, what would be the harm in wasting another two minutes?

"Oh, okay." Dana reached for the door handle, hating that she was acceding to his request. She'd have to watch herself around Patrick Connor. Vann was right when he said Patrick knew where all the "yes, of course" buttons were.

Out of the car, she rested against the door, folded her arms against her chest and waited.

Patrick ran the tip of his tongue over his lips. Dana realized her anger was fading and she was fixated on his mouth again. She looked sideways and tapped her fingers impatiently against her arm. At least she could make a good show of being irritated. He didn't need to know that she had a weakness for physical perfection.

He might use it against me.

"In there was nothing personal, Dana."

His words jerked her attention back to him. "It felt personal. To be exploited always feels personal."

"Well, I didn't mean for it to feel that way. I honestly am at my wit's end with some of those guys. But at the same time, I can't blame them. They're just doing what they were elected to do—representing the people who voted them in."

"They're on the school board, Patrick!" Her anger had returned, and she was glad of it. The response felt familiar and good and empowered her to ignore whatever this thing was she had for Patrick. "They're supposed to be representing the children's best interests."

"That's an idealistic approach." Patrick shook his head. "They're not heartless. The voters in Evans's district are older, with more property and fewer kids. They just don't see the value in investing in the schools.

If people hired you for a job, you'd do it the way they told you to do it, wouldn't you?"

"Not if it entailed shortchanging kids I wouldn't."

Patrick's laugh was hollow. "You know, if other people said that, I'd say they were full of crap, but I think you honestly mean it. Still, I have to accept the reality of the situation. This is simple arithmetic, dollars and cents. I have to take the paltry amount of tax dollars the county collects for the schools and stretch them to help the most students in the best possible way. I just can't justify spending instructional dollars on a mobile unit, especially when what I could afford wouldn't meet the needs."

"So why didn't you tell me yesterday how the board would react, Patrick? Before sending me in there?" She jabbed her thumb toward the board office. "Why send me in there to be ambushed or to make your case for you? Because I can tell you, based on what I heard tonight, unless somebody finds oil under the petunias, you aren't going to get that new school you've been lusting after any time soon."

Patrick shrugged. "I thought you'd understood. I didn't expect you'd read your presence as some sort of implied promise…."

He said something else, but she tuned him out, focusing instead on how similar his words, his tone, were to Marty's when he'd packed up to go after she'd told him she was pregnant. When she knew he didn't want them.

"Hey, are you in there?" Patrick waved a hand in front of her. "Are you even listening?"

Dana yanked her thoughts back from Marty and all the guys like him, guys who had bounced into her life for a month or two and then bounced right back out when Kate interfered with whatever plans they had. "Yes, I'm here. As for listening…" She rolled her eyes. "I get it. You're sorry. You didn't promise anything, and even if you had, you're not in any position to make good that promise. Gee, where have I heard that before? Oh, yeah, any human being cursed with a Y chromosome."

Patrick narrowed his eyes and studied her so intently that Dana laughed and looked away. He put a finger to her chin and brought her gaze back to his. "I—I don't know the guy you're talking about, but it's not me, Dana. And I don't make promises I can't keep. In fact, I make damn few promises because I want to follow through on each and every one."

She almost believed him. After all, he'd sailed right up there beside her yesterday to help her with Jakayla, getting stung in the process.

Or maybe she just wanted to believe him.

How could the lightest touch of a thumb and a forefinger on a tiny square inch of her skin undo her? Dana tried to swallow, found her throat parched with anticipation. He was so close.

Now his hand cupped her chin and his thumb grazed her lips. Dana hated that her mouth parted, beckoning him to kiss her. She hated that she wanted to lean in and meet him halfway.

Hormones. Just hormones. You can ignore them. You have to. Because you have Kate to think about, and casual sex is not an option.

She shut her eyes and attempted to gin up the strength to pull away. What would it take?

"That's great," she declared. "Now your two minutes are up. You have a meeting to finish, and I have to get home. Where *your* daughter is watching *my* daughter."

Her words worked as well as any spell ever uttered

by bad witches in fairy tales. Patrick's hand fell from her face and he stepped back.

Dana could have predicted the moment would end like this. She hadn't predicted, however, how great the hurt would be when it happened.

LISSA WAS PROPPED over a textbook at the kitchen table when Dana let herself in the back door. "Hey," Lissa said, "Kate's asleep already. You're back early, though. Dad never gets out of those board meetings until ten-thirty or eleven."

Dana dropped her keys on the counter and struggled not to think about Patrick. "I didn't see the need in staying."

Lissa shut the book. "Ooh. From the expression on your face, I'd say things didn't go well. Let me guess. Dad got on his 'only a new school will save us and we don't have money for anything else' soapbox."

Lissa's words drew Dana up short as she hung her purse on the hook by the door. "You know your father well. The meeting was a colossal waste of my time. I'm sorry that I had to ask you to keep Kate for me."

"No, no, I didn't mind in the slightest. She's an angel baby. There's leftover pizza from our supper. Want some?" Lissa crossed the kitchen to the fridge and began pulling the pizza box out. "I tried to get Kate to eat the bell peppers and the mushrooms, but she picked everything except the sausage and the pepperoni off."

"I should have warned you." Dana went to the sink to wash her hands. "Kate's on a green-bean jag these days. If a vegetable isn't a green bean, you can forget it."

"At least she'll eat those. I sit for some kids who will only eat chicken tenders and Pop-Tarts."

"Has your little brother outgrown food finickiness?"

"Christopher? He's on a growth spurt now, so he's eating us out of house and home. My stepdad says he must have a tapeworm. Want me to warm this up, or would you rather have it cold?"

"I'll nuke it. How on earth I made it through childhood without a microwave, I'll never understand." Dana grabbed a plate, dropped the slice of pizza on it and stuck it in the microwave. "Uh, if you don't mind me being nosy, how long have your parents been divorced?"

"Since I was little. I mean really little—so little, I can't even remember them being in the same house or my mom not being married to my stepdad. He's great, by the way, despite what Melanie says." Lissa glowered, and in that glower, Dana spotted a glimmer of Patrick in the girl.

"Melanie doesn't like him?" she prodded.

"No. But Aunt Suze says that's to be expected."

"Aunt Suze? You mean, your aunt is Suze Mitchell, the vice principal at the elementary school?"

Lissa nodded. "Yeah. I thought you knew that. I guess maybe not. I forget you're not from here. I can talk in shorthand to most people."

Dana stood there trying to process the information. The microwave beeped, and for a moment she let it beep on.

"You gonna get that?" Lissa asked.

"Yeah." Dana turned and retrieved the pizza. She recalled Suze requesting that Dana not mention her name to Patrick, her hesitancy about commenting on Patrick. "Suze didn't tell me that."

"Well, our family's complicated. Lots of skeletons. Bad blood. Grudges. Honestly, we should be on *Dr. Phil* or something."

Lissa appeared self-aware and self-conscious at the same time, struggling, Dana realized, to affect the cool detachment of someone much older than her eighteen years. Her agitated fiddling with the corner of the pizza box gave her away.

Dana succumbed to the bait before Lissa could shred the carton between her fingers. "So Suze is your…"

"My mom's sister. Maybe that's why Aunt Suze didn't say anything. See, Melanie's always sided with Dad against Mom and her family, and I…well, I don't think I chose sides or anything, but Dad can be so stubborn. When he gets his mind set, he doesn't change it." Lissa removed a slice of pizza from the carton. She inspected it for a long moment before starting to eat it, not seeming bothered by it being fridge-cold.

"Oh, yeah. I've found out that about him." Dana pulled out a chair and sat down beside Lissa. This whole conversation felt duplicitous. She was probing Lissa for information on her dad, the man Dana had very nearly kissed in the board of education parking lot.

Still Dana couldn't resist digging a little deeper, in the hope of figuring out why Patrick was…well, like Patrick. "You said skeletons. What sort of skeletons?"

Lissa wrinkled her nose. "Nothing criminal. Maybe I made it sound too dramatic. That's one thing Melanie's right about—sometimes I *am* a drama queen. But I guess I expected you knew. About Annabelle."

"Annabelle?" Who was she? Patrick's mistress? A girlfriend? The other woman?

"You don't know? Dad didn't tell you?" Lissa snorted, then took another bite of the pizza. "Just like Dad. Avoiding the hard conversations. Sheesh. Okay. Annabelle was my little sister."

"Was?" Cold comprehension settled along Dana's skin like a clammy blanket.

"Yeah. I don't remember her much. I was young—this was right before Mom and Dad got divorced. Annabelle had leukemia, and she got sick and she...died. When she was two and I was three."

CHAPTER SEVEN

DANA PUSHED AWAY the cooling slice of pizza. She thought about the little girl tucked in her princess sheets down the hall, thought about how it would be to see her sick, then sicker, then…nothing but a memory.

"What…is that…is that the reason your parents divorced?"

Lissa shrugged again. "I guess. Dad wouldn't say that. He blames Mom. But a lot of things were going on then, the way I hear it."

Dana fought the urge to run down the hall and check whether Kate was still breathing. It was the urge she always had after hearing about any child who'd died. She literally had to grip the chair bottom to keep herself in the kitchen. She blew out a sigh and gave up struggling to digest everything that Lissa had just recounted.

"I'm sorry, Lissa. I had no idea."

"How could you have? Dad didn't tell you. To be fair, it's not something you go around dropping into casual conversation. People treat you differently when they hear about it, like I'm going to break down and cry or something. Don't get me wrong—I get sad about it. But mostly, since I don't remember her that well, she's like a fairy tale. Except, every family squabble is really about her. You can bet that before the fight's over, someone will be screaming her name."

A sick realization hit Dana as she remembered how she'd brought up Kate's name earlier to drive away Patrick. That was why he freaked out about Kate. That's why he'd reacted the way he had when he'd seen her—and why Melanie had, too.

"What did she look like?" Dana whispered.

"Annabelle?" Lissa closed her eyes and twirled her hair around her index finger. "Really cute. She had curly dark hair—that is, before it all fell out—and these big blue eyes. They were the exact same shade of blue that my dad's eyes are—at least, that's what Mom says."

"Not like Kate?"

"No. Annabelle didn't look anything at all like Kate." Lissa concentrated before giving a firm shake of her head. "No, nothing at all."

Dana sat there for another long moment, not knowing what to say. How would she have done things differently with Patrick had she had this information? Why hadn't Suze told her?

Why hadn't Patrick?

Lissa shoved her chair back. "Well, it's getting late. I'll scoot."

"Wait, I haven't paid you." Dana made a move to get up, but Lissa waved her down, blushing deeply.

"Can I take my pay tonight in something besides cash?"

"Huh?" Dana squinted in confusion. "Sure. I guess. What do you want?"

"Well, remember I said that I was going to school to be a nurse? I'm going to the tech school."

"Yes. You want to work in pedes." Dana settled back in her chair. Outside, the neighbor's yappy dog started barking but blissfully stopped before the racket woke Kate.

"I, um, have to do an internship. And I was wondering… You know…"

Dana shook her head. "I don't follow."

"I sort of told my advisor that I could still get in my internship." Lissa flexed beringed fingers along the top of the dinette chair. "I screwed up. I was supposed to get my application in to the hospital, but I missed the deadline, and now Dad's on my back, and I'm not going to pass this course. Except, I could intern with you, right? And it's with kids, just like I wanted."

"With me." Dana couldn't help that her tone remained flat. "And your dad would approve?"

"Oh, he wants me to have an internship more than anything. So I can do it?"

Dana gritted her teeth. Just what she needed, an intern—her boss's daughter, no less—underfoot. Did she have a choice, though?

"Uh, I…guess. Sure."

"Great! Cool beans!" And then Lissa was out the door before Dana could stop her.

Dana sighed and turned back to the pizza. It was cold and congealed now, much like her stomach at the story Lissa had imparted.

To lose a daughter…

And then to have someone shove her daughter in your face without thought or feeling.

One thing was certain: she owed Patrick Connor more than just providing his daughter with an internship. And she'd deliver on that debt as soon as possible.

DANA DROVE into Logan Glass's graveled lot and shut off the engine. She was tempted to hit the ignition, slam the car in reverse and flee. But no. The least she could do was apologize to this man for anything she might have unthinkingly said to offend him.

She'd gotten up a half-hour early to do this. Rushed a sleepy Kate through her Cheerios, nearly forgotten Kate's beloved Pink Doll and skipped any attempt to rescue her hair from what was looking like the Bad Hair Day From Hell.

Well, a clean conscience was supposed to be the world's softest pillow. She could use a good night's sleep after last night's tossing and turning.

She heaved a sigh and opened the door. Not sure where to find Patrick, Dana tried the office. No one was at the front counter. She waited to see if any of the workers would notice her arrival.

Her wait was rewarded after a familiar chambray shirt appeared in the door off the garage bays. "Sorry for the delay. How can we help you?" And then the words came to an abrupt end as Patrick realized who he was offering to help.

"Hi." Her throat closed up.

"Hi," he replied. "I gather this isn't about a windshield."

Dana shook her head. "I wanted to apologize."

"About last night? Let's just forget it. Chalk it up to good intentions gone awry."

"No. About…something else."

Why was it so hard to say? She'd lain awake the whole night practicing her words, perfecting her apology.

"Okay. Uh, my office, then?" Patrick gestured to a tiny glassed-in space behind the front counter. "We'll have some privacy there."

Dana preceded him in. Patrick followed her, then shut the door and circled around her.

She debated whether to take the chair he proffered, but decided against it after he elected to remain standing. She propped herself up against the chair back, though, for added support when his smile was cool and impersonal.

"Lissa told me about…" Dana couldn't get the words out.

Patrick raised his eyebrows and inclined his head, waiting. "About what?"

"Annabelle."

If she'd pointed a gun at him, he would have looked no more shocked than he did at the sound of his daughter's name. He reached out a hand to grip the bookshelves behind him, and the knuckles on that hand went white.

"Oh," he said. His tone was curt. "What does that have to do with an apology?"

Dana wasn't clear what she'd expected, but it certainly wasn't this.

"Um, well, I wanted to apologize about Kate. I mean, she obviously causes you…difficulty." She was drowning; nothing was coming out the way she wanted it to. "I'm sorry. I didn't know, or I wouldn't have brought Kate around."

"Listen, you lose a daughter you can't expect that the world will stop showing you baby pictures, okay?" Patrick snapped. His blue eyes turned cold. "It happened a long time ago, and I've seen hundreds of kids since then, lots and lots of toddlers. You don't have to apologize for anything."

"But I feel that I do. I unthinkingly barged in on your birthday, with my daughter, which I wouldn't have done had I'd known. And then last night, when I said—"

"I get the picture."

"Well." Dana rubbed at her forehead. "That's it, then…what I wanted to say. I just wish someone had told me. Suze at least. So I wouldn't have stuck my size-eight shoe into my size-ten mouth." She pivoted to go.

"I figured Suze Mitchell wouldn't have waited this long to fill you in on what an unfeeling bastard I am. That whole family likes to blame me for everything."

Dana stopped and whirled back. "Suze hasn't said anything of the sort. Only that you were a good guy…but you had issues. Well, I wish she'd told me what those issues were."

"You think it's helpful to spread gossip?"

"No. Besides, cluing someone in about a painful loss isn't spreading gossip. It's consideration, compassion."

"Compassion. That's rich. That family has a strange idea of compassion. Siding with my wife when she has an affair while my daughter is dying? Oh, yeah. They know a lot about compassion. They wrote the book on it." Patrick's face was taut with rage. "My fault. They say it was my fault because I couldn't—" he made quotation marks in the air with his fingers "'—be there' for Jenny. I couldn't 'listen' to Jenny. Well, hell, who was there to listen to me? Not Jenny. She was with her support group guy. He was supporting her, all right." His chuckle was harsh.

"Look." Dana held up her hand. "I'm sorry. This has obviously stirred some bad memories for you. I just wanted to apologize for anything I might have unwittingly done to hurt you."

"Which you hadn't until now. People can be so well-meaning. But they pick and pry and poke. They're like drivers on I-75, rubbernecking a wreck, thinking, 'Thank God it's not me' before they hit the accelerator and speed back to their normal lives."

"I'm just trying to make amends."

"For what? Having a little girl when I don't?" Patrick made an exaggerated shrug. "That's the way the cookie crumbled for me."

"You say that as though you've put the event behind you, but you haven't. I didn't want to hurt anyone, and if I did, I just want to apologize." Dana couldn't understand why she felt it so imperative to show him she hadn't meant malice.

"So now you view me as someone wounded and hurt and with—how did Suze say it—issues? But you've made it clear that up till now you thought I was some kind of calculating bean counter, more interested in preventing lawsuits than protecting the students. What? You couldn't endow me with a heart unless I had some personal tragedy that makes me, let me guess, hate all kids and want 'em to die of mold?"

Dana's grip on the chair wasn't from uncertainty now but from anger. "Listen, I drove out here as a courtesy, as one parent to another, to say that I was sorry. As far as I'm concerned, you're still a bean counter. I can't figure out, though, how you can still be that way after you've lost—" She slapped her hand over her mouth, not believing the words that had just slipped out.

"Oh, I get it. Why didn't I catch it earlier?" Patrick snapped. "This is simply some sort of manipulation to convince me to spend money on something *you* consider a priority, when you obviously can't look at the bigger picture. You're trying to guilt me into spending the money. Well, it won't work. Unless and until I see there's money that would be better spent on enriching the coffers of a mold abatement company or the manufacturer of a mobile unit—which I won't, not with textbooks and paper to buy and teachers to pay—I won't be moved. Not by you or anybody, and you do have some apologizing to do if that's your motivation for driving out here."

Dana gasped, sputtered for a moment or so, the words she was struggling to utter not remotely intelligible. She veered around and made for the exit. "I am sorry," she snapped, pushing on the door. "I'm sorry I thought you were remotely human."

PATRICK'S KNEES RIVALED soggy macaroni noodles in strength as the office door banged shut behind Dana. He rounded the desk unsteadily and dropped into his desk chair. For once, he didn't mind the spring that poked into his back.

He rested his elbows on the desk and dropped his face into his hands. His breakfast threatened to rise back up.

All this time, and the mention of Annabelle's name could still send him.

All this time, and people still didn't get it, still couldn't understand how hard talking about her was.

Patrick rubbed his mouth, astonished that the pain felt so fresh. It wasn't like people didn't ask him about Annabelle. It wasn't as though he didn't see happy families every day. But somehow he'd managed to cage that demon pain, stuff it down where it couldn't hurt him. If he just didn't think about it, he didn't have to deal with it. But Dana…Dana had yanked him back to all those years ago.

She had meant well. Some part of him had realized that when he'd uttered those hateful things.

But Patrick had learned over the years that just because people's intentions were good didn't mean the hurt was any less.

Annabelle. Annabelle.

Sometimes when he concentrated and tried to remember, he couldn't conjure the sound of her voice. That first time when he couldn't recall her lisp, her giggle, he couldn't breathe. It was as if he was losing her all over again. If he couldn't remember her, did that mean she was fading from existence bit by bit?

Patrick fumbled for the bottom drawer of his desk, pushed aside the empty envelopes and file folders he'd put there to hide the real contents of the drawer. He glanced out his office windows, just to make certain no one was looking. His fingers touched cool glass, and his chest eased.

Then he pulled it out and placed it in front of him on his desk. Once wouldn't hurt. Then he could put it away until he needed it again.

He ran his fingers along the glass, wishing that its coolness could soothe him the way the warm reassurance of holding his daughter's hand had.

He drank it in then, the comfort it offered him. There she was, trapped behind the glass in color, whole, healthy, alive. The last studio portrait they'd had done of her before they'd found out that Annabelle was a loan from God due back way too soon.

And then, as he always did when he had to take out her picture to remember her, he sobbed.

CHAPTER EIGHT

"WHY DIDN'T YOU TELL ME?" Dana asked Suze. Suze still seemed nonplussed over the way Dana had come in, banging the outer office door.

"Whoa, girl! Tell you what? What on earth ate you?"

Dana snatched up her time card. The time clock stamped it with a *cachunk* that echoed in the empty outer office. She tried to slip the card back into the rack, but it fluttered from her nervous fingers to the floor.

After scooping it up, she carefully replaced it before she answered Suze.

"You said you had history with Patrick Connor. You didn't bother telling me that 'history' meant you were family."

Suze sagged against the receptionist's desk. "*Was* family. He's not family anymore."

"You could have given me a heads-up, Suze!"

The door opened and the receptionist popped her head in. "Hey, Suze, can you cover for me? I swear, just ten minutes. Jessica forgot her homework again, and I have to run home and get it."

Suze nodded and waved her out, then returned her attention to Dana. As soon as the door shut, she beckoned Dana into her office. "But can you hold it down? I've got to leave my door open, and in a minute, that outer office will be crawling with humanity. After the board members finish trashing you for stomping out of last night's meeting, I don't need Harrison to hear about you going off like a bottle rocket on me. You're a good nurse, Dana, much better than we deserve. I'd like to keep you around."

"I didn't stomp out." Dana sagged into a chair. "I guess I did. He just made me so mad. They all made me mad. Bean counters, the lot of them."

Suze perched on the corner of her desk so that she could maintain an eye on the outer office. "And it would have made a difference if I'd told you Patrick was my sister's ex?"

"It would have made a difference if I'd known about Annabelle."

Suze sucked in a breath, and Dana cursed herself for lobbing another stink bomb at Suze, in much the same way she'd lobbed it at Patrick.

A conversation between two teachers filtered from outside Suze's door, and the phone began to ring. The vice principal grabbed up the handset on the first buzz. She answered the question, then put the receiver down, only to have the phone ring as soon as she did. Suze rolled her eyes and picked up the receiver again.

The hiss of air brakes signaled that the first bus had arrived, and Dana watched through Suze's window as kids started spilling out of the big yellow bus.

She rose to her feet and began to leave, but Suze, deep in conversation with an irate parent, surfaced to motion for Dana to stop.

Dana waited for a moment in the doorway. Teachers lined up at the time clock, in a hurry to get out the door, fussing about the unexpected early arrival of the bus.

Now Harrison arrived on the scene, bombastic and

booming. "You should all be in your rooms! Am I going to have to make sign-in times fifteen minutes earlier?" His pronouncement sent the teachers scuttling all the faster.

He turned to Dana. "And you! Ms. Wilson, those children will be finished with breakfast and waiting on their morning medications. Why are you dawdling? Tired after your late night? I heard about your speech before the board last night. I am not happy. Not happy at all."

Suze spoke up in Dana's defense. "Uh, Mr. Harrison, I asked her to wait. It's about a, uh, project I want her help with."

"And where is my receptionist?" Harrison's question rattled off the cinder-block walls of the office just as the hapless woman scurried back through the door.

Dana hesitated, not sure whether to go or stay. She glanced at Suze, who jerked her head almost imperceptibly and began following her.

In the hall, engulfed in an incoming tide of students, Suze said, "I'm sorry. I guess it wasn't fair to not give you some sort of warning. What happened?"

Mindful of inquisitive ears, Dana kept her explanation short and sweet. They arrived at her clinic door to see she did indeed have a line forming.

Dana knelt and gave a jaundiced inspection of the lock, but today saw no gum jamming the tumblers. She slid in her key, opened the door and got the morning medications going.

Over the heads of kids swilling down their meds, Dana ended her brief recounting with, "I just wish you'd told me, Suze. Maybe…" Dana let her eyes wander. "I felt like an idiot. I shouldn't have gone to his office. But I just wanted—"

"Girl, when it comes to Patrick Connor, there's no

getting it right." Suze closed her eyes and shook her head. "Nothing you could say, nothing you could do. If you'd told me you were planning on taking Kate with you that first night, I probably—I don't know. Maybe not. Sometimes, I admit, I forget that Patrick hasn't moved on, whereas the rest of us have."

"He was so hostile." Dana chewed on her bottom lip and sent the last kid out the door. "It was like, I don't know, a volcano going off."

"Been that way since Annabelle died. He *looks* like he's got it all together. But you mention that girl around him—or mention Jenny, especially Jenny—and whew! Mount Vesuvius all over again."

"What's the story? He said that Jenny…" Dana trailed off, not exactly sure how to ask tactfully if Suze's sister had had an affair.

"I know what he said. I've heard it all before. He said Jenny had an affair while Annabelle was dying."

"Did she?"

"The question is, did she even have a husband anymore to cheat on? Patrick wouldn't budge from the hospital, and when he did, he wouldn't talk, wouldn't get involved in any therapy, wouldn't go to support group meetings with Jenny, wouldn't admit for the longest time that Annabelle wasn't going to get better. He was so deep in denial. He said…he accused Jen of going into counseling so she could learn how to forget Annabelle ever lived."

"Patrick never went to counseling?" Dana ran her hand through her hair. "God, if something happened to Kate, they'd have to wheel me off immediately to a padded room. I'd need all the counseling I could get."

"I felt sorry for the kids. Melanie was old enough to know what was going on, but not old enough to understand that we couldn't save Annabelle. And she was Patrick's little shadow. She always blamed her mom for the divorce. When Mel turned fourteen, she actually went to live with Patrick, which killed Jenny. It was losing a daughter all over again."

"And Lissa?"

From the doorway came Lissa's voice. "Lissa's just always been in the middle."

Both Dana and Suze jumped, startled by Lissa's appearance.

"Lissa, how long—"

"Long enough. It's okay, Aunt Suze. This is all ancient history. Besides, Dad reamed me a new one for—how'd he put it?" She made quotation marks in the air and looked so much like her father when she did that Dana gasped. "Sharing our family business? Yeah. That's how he put it."

She threw herself into the chair beside Dana's desk and shot Dana a rueful smile. "Bet you wished you'd never knocked on our door, huh?"

Dana considered the question, though she knew Lissa had meant it rhetorically. She could think of no way to answer it without sounding either condescending or like a complete liar, so she let it pass. "What are you doing here?"

"My internship, remember?"

Dana smothered a curse. She hadn't remembered— or at least, she hadn't figured on Lissa's internship starting this soon.

Suze cleared her throat. "Uh, Lissa, you're doing an internship here?"

"Yeah. Why not? Dana said I could."

"Oh, boy." Suze shook her head and about-faced out the door.

"Something *else* I should know?" Dana called after her pointedly.

"Yeah. Stock up on lots of bandages and whatcha-macallits—sutures. You're gonna need 'em."

"Huh?" Dana followed her to the clinic door and poked her head around. "Suze?"

But Suze didn't turn. She just shook her head again and kept on walking.

Dana retreated into the clinic. "Now, what was that about?"

Lissa shrugged. She began poking around in cabinets, pulling things out. Dana halted her plundering with a firm hand on a cabinet door. "Hey. First rule of internship. Don't go messing in my supplies."

"Just checking. Sorry. I get the picture." Lissa adopted the stiff posture of an offended teenager.

Don't tick off the boss's daughter.

The mental caution gave Dana an idea on how to make the best use of her free labor.

"Can you do Excel spreadsheets?"

"Yeah, sure. Learned how in my computer classes in high school, and I had to take a course at the tech school. They're a breeze."

"Okay. I have some entries that I want you to make." She set Lissa to work inputting more of the asthma test results that she'd gotten behind on the day before.

It kept the girl quiet for all of thirty seconds. "Hey. These are the mold tests, aren't they?"

"Uh, yeah." Now Dana wondered if she should have assigned her that particular project.

"You're not going to accept Dad's no for a final answer, are you?"

"Oh, that." Dana harrumphed. Despite the closed door, she heard Principal Harrison's self-important reminders to the janitorial staff on the proper way to store a broom. She pitied the custodians, and was glad she wasn't the focus of Harrison's attention. "I've got to think on it. Right now I'm at an impasse. If I were back in Savannah, I'd go to my gym and swim about a hundred laps, and the answer would go 'Bing!'" Dana sighed.

"You swim?" Lissa.

"Well, I used to before I moved to Logan."

"The motel by the interstate has a heated indoor pool," Lissa told her. "You pay a monthly fee, and you can use the pool and the weight room. It's cool."

Dana brightened. "I hadn't heard about that." Another thing Suze had failed to mention.

"Well, if you need some quiet time, I could watch Kate for you. The best times to go are in the evenings, after seven-thirty or so. Tonight's good because it's a weeknight and the schoolkids don't hang out there. Plus, I don't work on Wednesdays and Thursdays."

Dana chuckled. "You starting a franchise with this babysitting business or what?"

Lissa's cheeks pinkened. "I could use the money, that's for certain. Dad still won't cosign my car loan, and I'm having to save up for a bigger down payment."

Dana let her mind drift back to how good a swim in warm, relaxing waters felt, how much stress she could burn off, not to mention calories. Lissa had kept Kate without incident the night before, and by eight o'clock, bathtime was done and Kate tucked in bed. How much harm could there be in stealing an hour or so to swim?

"Okay," she said. "But only for an hour, and it will have to be after I put Kate to bed. Be at my place around a quarter to eight. And maybe we'll do this once a week if I like the pool. Deal?"

Lissa beamed. "Deal!"

PATRICK DIDN'T BOTHER with the diving board, just swam laps. He attempted to focus on his breathing, his form, but swimming didn't work its usual magic. Thoughts of the day's confrontations, first with Dana, then Lissa, kept intruding.

He felt like crap about losing it with Dana. She'd been trying to be nice, trying to be helpful, probably egged on by whatever Lissa had told her.

That was what steamed him. He picked up his pace, hitting the end of the pool quicker than he'd anticipated, before flipping around and heading back. Lissa of all people knew how he liked to keep that portion of his life private. So why had she trotted out the story for Dana? Had it been an attention-seeking bid? Lord knows he loved Lissa, but she did demand the spotlight.

"Mind if I join you?" A woman's voice floated through the water.

Damn. Now he was hallucinating about hearing Dana's voice. With a glance out the corner of his eye before he turned his head, Patrick discerned the shapely form of a woman in a one-piece. He swam even faster, in an effort to burn off the irritation he felt about his sanctuary being invaded. He'd purposefully picked this time for his weekly laps because no one else swam then.

If he'd hated the way he'd lost it with Dana, he definitely regretted unloading on Lissa. Whatever fences they'd mended were probably torn down now. She'd just sat there, let him blast her, and all she'd done was tap the toes of the hideously expensive boots he'd caved in and bought for her birthday.

In front of him, he heard the diving board squeak as the lady prepared for her dive. He reached the end of the pool just as she entered the water, and he couldn't help but admire the low-key but perfect form as her lithe body cut through the blue waters of the pool. Whoever the woman was, she hadn't been paddling around in the kiddie pool for a while.

If Lissa hadn't told Dana, then he wouldn't have been—well—ambushed. Patrick had to be *prepared* to talk about Annabelle.

He leaned against the wall of the pool, treading water, as he watched the woman. Like her dive, her strokes weren't showy, but they revealed good technique. Her hair was tucked into a swimmer's cap, and the dark blue swimsuit clung to her curves in a way that left just enough to his imagination. Long, lean legs powered through the water, form beautifully following function.

That's what Dana's legs would look like.

The woman arrived at the opposite end of the pool, touched the end and did a smooth somersault to turn back toward Patrick. He continued to watch her. He knew of no one in Logan who could swim that well, or was that interested in swimming as a sport.

Now the woman was a lane over, a quick couple of strokes away. She popped up out of the water, her head thrown back in a laugh. "Wow!"

Dana. Patrick froze at the realization that it *was* her. His body began to sink in the water, and he gripped the diving board above his head to keep afloat.

"Dana? What—"

She whipped her head around. Her own shock was evident in the surprised O her mouth formed.

"Patrick? What are you doing here?"

CHAPTER NINE

DANA MUST HAVE taken his flabbergasted silence for an answer of sorts. She streaked for the pool ladder and jumped out of the water as if it were boiling hot.

Patrick hauled himself up over the side of the pool and padded to the chaise longue she stood by. She wasn't looking at him but was instead pulling on a cover-up. "Hey," he said, "I don't know how you came to be here, but this is my regular time."

Dana stopped in mid-yank of the cover-up. "Oh. Lissa."

"What about Lissa?"

"It was Lissa who suggested I swim tonight at this time."

He swore and shifted his focus to the No Life Guard On Duty sign. "I have no idea what Lissa was thinking."

She sank onto the chaise longue. "I can guess."

The pool filter kicked on and filled the room with a low hum. Water lapped against the sides of the empty pool. Out of the water, Patrick suddenly didn't know what to do with his arms. "I wasn't aware you swam."

"Yeah. High school swim team. College, too. I don't compete anymore, of course."

"College, uh. Me, too." Something about this unexpected thing they had in common flummoxed him more than it ought to have.

"I should have guessed Lissa was up to something, what with her being so specific about the best swim times. But I figured it was because of her schedule, when she could watch Kate." Dana flinched but hurried on with her next words. "I thought Lissa was trying to butter me up to give her good marks on her internship."

"Internship? What internship?"

"Lissa's internship. She started with me today. She said you wanted her…" Dana trailed off, and Patrick saw realization dawn on her face. "You didn't know about the internship."

"Not a whisper." Patrick rubbed a hand along the back of his neck, then flung the water droplets he'd collected to the cement floor. "Can you hand me one of those towels?" He pointed to the stack on the other side of Dana's chair.

She grabbed one and held it out for him. Patrick managed a smile as he accepted it. He dried himself off with the white fluffy terry cloth, pulled up a folding chair and sat down. The scrape of the metal on the floor echoed through the cavernous room.

"What made you offer Lissa an internship?" he asked.

"I thought—"

"That I'd expect it? As the board chair?"

Dana averted her eyes. "Well, it wasn't *just* that. I like Lissa. She's sweet. A little scattered, but sweet. And she's genuinely good with kids."

Her ability to find something positive in a girl who'd put both of them in a series of awkward situations in short order gratified Patrick.

"Thank you," he managed to say. "She needed the internship. I was planning on white-knuckling it, letting her reap what she sowed…but thank you."

"Don't thank me yet."

"So, you swim. Regularly?"

Dana narrowed her eyes at his clumsy change of subject. "Are we being all grown-up and adult here?"

Her question confused him for a moment. "You mean, me trying to talk to you?"

"Yeah. Just this morning you made it abundantly clear how you felt about me. What's changed?"

Patrick studied the rough cement at his feet and clicked his teeth while he struggled to figure out how to answer. He raised his head. "I could say the internship with Lissa. But the truth is, I don't know. Can't people understand how a guy can lose it when they go poking around in things that aren't any of their business?"

Dana's jaw tightened, and for a brief second, he expected her to spring from the chair. She surprised him by saying, "Fair enough."

If he was expecting her to elaborate, she didn't. She stared at him to the point that he had to look away. Still she was silent, not saying anything, not assisting him in the least. Finally, he muttered, "I can't talk about her."

"Who?"

"Who? Who do you think? Venus rising from the sea?" He could barely contain himself. "You want me to say it? Say her name? *Annabelle*. I can't talk about Annabelle."

Dana sat still, not making any more moves to leave. "Okay. I can understand that. But having all that pain doesn't give you the right to accuse me of manipulating you. That wasn't fair, Patrick."

"I know. I regretted my words later. Which is why I was making an effort to be—how'd you put it—all grown-up about tonight."

"What about Lissa?"

"What about her?" Patrick asked.

"You reamed her out for telling me. That wasn't fair, either."

Patrick raked his fingers through wet hair. "I know. If you're attempting to prove that I'm an all-around first-class jerk, well, you're too late. I've already convinced myself of that."

"It would help," she said in a quiet, neutral voice, "if you didn't force people to guess."

"About my life? About what happened?" He scoffed and shook his head. "Yeah. Maybe. But you know what? Sometimes I'm selfish, Dana, and I'm not always thinking what'll make it easier on other people. How about this? How about after you lose a kid, you let me know if making it easier on other people is at the top of *your* list."

She started to speak but then closed her mouth. She jerked up her canvas bag, and walked past him.

"Wait. Dammit. This is not…wait. Let's start over and I'll try to be a grown-up," he yelled after her.

Dana glanced back over her shoulder. "Maybe it's me who's not being the grown-up. In the medical profession we have the dictum 'First do no harm.' And obviously my presence brings up memories you'd rather not have."

"Stay. Swim. Please. You're not harming me. This is what happens when people bring up…her. It's why I can't talk about her. It's why Jenny and I…" He sank back in his chair. Had he really been going to assume part of the blame for Jenny hauling off and having an affair? It wasn't his fault.

But something he'd said had made Dana turn around and close the gap between them. She didn't speak. He was afraid she might, afraid she would seize upon his words as a signal to explore more of what he'd meant.

Hell if I know what *I meant.*

Dana locked eyes with him for a long moment. Then she set her bag down and stripped off her cover-up. He couldn't tear his gaze from the expression of challenge on her face, not even to take in the body he'd admired earlier.

"Okay," she said. "I'll stay. For now."

He watched her as she padded in bare feet back to the diving board. She arced through the air and hit the surface with a minimum of splash, then cut through the water with intention.

Patrick sighed and stood up. Feeling more alone than ever, he joined her in the pool.

LISSA WAS WAITING for Dana in the kitchen when she got home. A tension in Lissa's frame belied the casual way she had her chin propped on the palm of her hand as she studied a biology textbook.

"Have a good time?" Lissa asked even before Dana could hang up her coat.

"Hmm. Let's see. Did I?" Dana ditched her purse and her keys. "Or did you have something else in mind when you set me up to run into your dad?"

At least Lissa had the grace to look ashamed. "I thought you could talk, you know? You swim. He swims. You get together. He realizes what a jerk he's been." She bit her lip. "It didn't go down like that, huh?"

Dana pulled out a chair at the kitchen table. She dropped her head into her hands and sighed. How had it gone? An hour of tense, silent laps definitely hadn't been the therapeutic swim she'd hoped for.

"That bad?" Lissa prompted.

Dana regarded her. "Lissa, why? What on earth possessed you?"

The girl picked at a hangnail. "I dunno. You like him, right?"

"Like him? I barely know him. And he's your father. It feels weird, you setting me up. He's your *father.*"

"Yeah. He is. And he's not getting any younger. We're about to be gone, Dana. Melanie and me. I've got one more year at Heart of Georgia Tech and then I'm off to the big bad world for a real job. And Melanie's husband can't keep turning down job transfers. Mom's got her husband and Christopher. But Dad...Dad hasn't got *anybody.*"

Dana scrutinized Lissa. Was she telling the truth or spinning a tale? This was, after all, the girl who had sided against Patrick in earlier family squabbles. "So how do I fit in? And what makes you think you're any good at all at playing Cupid?"

"You're about the only woman around here Dad hasn't dated and dumped."

Dana didn't bother to suppress a sarcastic chuckle. "Wow. What a recommendation for your dad. Pencil me in for next Friday night."

"No, listen. Half the women in Logan are either over sixty or under thirty. The rest of 'em are married, or Dad's already dated them."

"So he does date."

"If you can call it that. Takes them out a couple of times to eat and catch a movie at the multiplex in Dublin or Vidalia, then boom. Suddenly, they're leaving messages on his answering machine. He just hits the delete button without waiting for the message to even finish. Not exactly the way to keep that loving feeling."

Dana watched Lissa clasp and unclasp her hands as

she said her piece. Reaching over and spreading her hands over Lissa's, she said, "He's not ready, Lissa. And it's not your job to make him ready. When he's able to let go of the past and move on, he will. Trying to fix him up the way you did tonight will simply backfire on you."

Lissa nodded, her bottom lip quivering. "I know. I thought that he liked you. He was interested—I could tell. I just want him to be happy and have a good time and not be such a wet blanket."

Now Dana's chuckle contained no sarcasm. "Oh, honey, I am definitely not in the market for a man. Believe you me, I've been there, done that, and I have no desire to repeat the trip. I had my fill with my ex-husband, not to mention all the male disasters who followed him. When you're a single mother, things get complicated. And guys understand that."

Lissa closed her book. "Complicated? *Complicated* is a code word for too-chicken."

"I agree. All the men I've dated *are* chicken."

Lissa shoved her chair back with no concern for Dana's newly polished floor. "Not them. *You.*"

Cheeky demon, isn't she? Dana mused.

"I'm not chicken. Hey, I stuck out the dating game. When anyone suggested I meet someone, I did. But after a while, even the dimmest bulb gets a glimmer."

"Let me guess. They were all blind dates." Lissa was stacking things in a pile now, and Dana marveled at how the girl could total out an entire kitchen table in less than an evening. What would she be like to live with?

"So? I'm a single mom, Lissa. I can't go trolling for men in bars or online. I have to consider Kate. I have to *know* that any man I get involved with is—"

"Good father material? Maybe that's your problem. You were already planning the wedding before the first kiss. Didn't you just want some fun?"

Fun. Since when could a single mom have the luxury of fun? Agreeing to a date became a complex calculation of risk versus payoff.

"If you hadn't been chicken, you would have gotten out there. Joined some clubs, gone to a seminar or enrolled in some classes or something. Blind dates? Dr. Phil would say you were just going through the motions."

Oh, God, a teenager armed with a master's degree from a television talk-show shrink. And she'd agreed to let the girl intern with her.

"Lissa, my private life is mine. Let's leave it at that, okay?"

Dana's tone was harsh, harsher than she would have liked. Lissa's face crumpled, and the self-aware, self-taught young woman dissolved into a girl far less certain.

"Guess I kind of blew the babysitting gig, huh? And the internship?"

Dana sat back in her chair. "You think I'd take away your internship?"

"Well, I screwed up."

Dana couldn't answer in the face of the misery oozing from Lissa. She rose from her chair and crossed to the sink. She ran the cold water for a drink while she formulated her response. "The screwup came from you not being honest. About tonight, and about the internship, which your dad knew nothing about."

Behind her, Lissa's feet shuffled. "It won't happen again."

"Darn tootin' it won't. Don't lie to me. I can deal with the truth any day. But…" The memory of Marty's lies, and the well-meaning lies of all those blind dates who wouldn't turn into fathers, blasted her.

It's not you, they'd said. *It's me.* But it hadn't been just them. It had been their inability to commit to Kate.

"I promise. I won't let you down." Lissa was at the door now, apparently not wanting to push the matter.

"Lissa? One more thing."

"Yes?" Lissa sounded wary as she waited for Dana to carefully dry her hands.

"Your dad. Is he there *every* Wednesday night?"

"Not every—" She broke off. "Well, most Wednesdays and Thursdays. But it's not like he's got the place reserved. I mean, the pool's big enough for both of you, right?"

Dana didn't answer. After tonight, the Pacific Ocean didn't seem big enough for the two of them.

CHAPTER TEN

PATRICK DUCKED TO avoid November's fierce rain and jogged toward the school door. He'd almost made it, when he caught sight of pink legs sticking out of the storm sewer drain in the school's driveway.

Long pink legs ending in nurse clogs.

He turned around. Heading up the sidewalk, he shouted, "Dana? What's going on?"

If she heard him, she didn't acknowledge it. Now Patrick was close enough to see that the heavy steel grate was slid back so that Dana could get half her body into the opening. Her feet waggled in the air as she scooted forward another inch or so.

"Dana?"

He knelt beside her. Water from the driveway sluiced down and had to be making Dana feel she was almost drowning. She seemed mindless to it as it gurgled past her.

Her voice, when she answered, echoed in the sewer. "Shh. You'll scare him."

"Scare who?" The hairs on Patrick's neck prickled. He examined the size of the grate. No way could a kid have gotten trapped in there, not unless the grate had been removed.

Which it had. So who had moved it? And when?

Dana didn't respond to his question directly, just

commenced crooning. "Come here, sweetie. No, no, don't be afraid. Come to me." She edged in farther, an "Oof!" escaping from her as she stretched for whatever it was. "Come here, baby. That's right."

"Who are you talking to?" The rain drilled him in the back, bulletlike, especially when coupled with the sound it made against the metal breezeway leading to the school.

"Blast. I almost had him." She pulled back. Mud caked her scrubs. Her hair, in its untidy ponytail, was drenched and limp. Dana wiped at her eyes and regarded Patrick.

"Are you good with dogs?" she inquired.

"Huh? A dog's down there?"

"A puppy. He's scared, and I think he's hurt. For the first time in my life, I'm not tall enough to do something. Can you help?"

"I'll try." Now he stretched out beside her. Water soaked into his clothes, making him cold and clammy. With a sucked-in breath to prepare himself, he poked his head into the blackness.

"Do you see him? He's on a ledge of some sort, just out of reach. Every time I almost get him, he scuttles back."

Patrick saw something, even if it didn't exactly resemble a dog. In the dim light of the sewer, two black eyes twitched from side to side. He could detect no real shape, just the nervous eyes, but he heard a whimper.

Bracing himself, Patrick reached toward the sound. Immediately, the eyes zipped back into the dimness. Small white teeth bared themselves. He drew back, nearly hitting his head in the process.

Now Dana was sticking her head into the opening. "Did you get him?"

"Not yet. He growled at me."

"Afraid of a little pooch?" she teased.

"That thing has teeth and Lord only knows what else." But Patrick reached out his hand again, this time touching soaked fur and shivering pup.

He couldn't quite get hold of the dog, though, not a good enough grasp to be sure he wouldn't drop the animal into sewer. Below the ledge, water burbled down noisily as if through an economy-size bathtub drain. That the puppy hadn't already been washed away was a sheer miracle.

"Extracting him is going to require both of us, I think," Patrick declared. "I'll grab him, but you have to be ready to catch him if he wiggles free."

"Got it. On three?" She smiled at Patrick, and he became aware of their closeness, the way their hips bumped, the way their legs lay nearly touching.

"On three," he agreed.

He stretched out his hand anew, only to stop when Dana asked, "One-two-three and grab, or one-two-grab?"

Patrick hesitated. As he did, the puppy drew a little closer. Now Patrick could detect a tiny wet nose snuffling in his direction.

"You choose," he offered. He let the dog sniff his fingers.

"One-two-three and grab," Dana said. Once more she was beside him, her warmth permeating him the way the rainwater had.

He studied her for a moment, saw mud on her cheek and her teeth catching her bottom lip as she concentrated. Dana met his eyes.

"What?"

"You're crazy, you know that?"

"Hey, who's the one who volunteered to help?"

"The crazier one," Patrick conceded. "Isn't that what you're thinking?"

Her smile broadened. "Just saying. Now can we do this?"

Patrick made the count and lunged for the puppy. He caught the animal by the scruff of the neck. For a heart-stopping moment full of the dog's terrified squeals, he was afraid he had dropped him.

Dana, however, had been right on cue. Her hands came up to cup the bedraggled body of the little guy. Together, they hauled him over the drain and began wriggling backward in concert. Patrick scooped him closer to his body, feeling Dana's fingers follow.

In the gray daylight, he regarded his find. A tiny puppy he could easily cup in two hands shivered against Patrick's chest. The pup's black hair was curly despite being as soaked as Patrick was.

"Poor baby," Dana said.

He held the puppy up. "He's not much to look at, is he?"

"He's cute," she protested. "Aren't you a dog person?"

"I had a collie for years. This critter needs a serious bath. How'd he get in there?"

"Beats me. One of the kids ran in telling me about it, and I raced out to look. Sure enough, there he was."

The rain had slacked off, but the runoff hadn't, and it still flooded around them. Patrick rose on unsteady feet.

Dana stood, as well. "I'm pretty sure I noticed a cut on him. Carry him in and I'll check." She began walking to the school.

"Oh," Patrick said, following her. "Now you're a vet, too?"

"No, but a cut's a cut."

Patrick realized she was shivering as badly as the dog. "Why didn't you bring a coat?" he asked as he waited for her to hold open the door.

"I have more scrubs, but not another coat."

"Good thinking." He surveyed his own totaled jeans and jacket. "Well, I'll have to go home and change."

Dana fished in her pocket and pulled out a dripping pair of keys. Just as she was about to insert the key in the lock, Principal Harrison's voice resounded from the other end of the hall, instructing, with excruciating precision, the custodians on how to decorate the school Christmas tree. She stiffened, then redoubled her efforts to get the door unlocked.

"Hurry! He might spot us!" Dana shoved the door open and gave Patrick an encouraging push through the doorway. She slammed the door behind her.

"What now?" Patrick felt the dog jiggle in his grasp. "No, boy, hold on."

"Harrison is not a dog person. I don't know what kind of person he is, but he doesn't like dogs or cats or gerbils—or people, for that matter. I don't want him to find out I'm treating a dog in the clinic. He'd tell me to take the animal to the pound."

She was opening cabinets as she said all this, then banging them shut after plucking items out of first one, then another.

"You didn't tell Harrison you were rescuing a dog?"

Dana shook her head. "Nope."

"But you trusted me enough not to bust you?"

"I was desperate." She dumped Betadine and a tube of ointment onto the counter by the sink and began filling the sink with warm water. "Here. Put the little guy in the water."

Patrick did as he was bidden. The dog sensed the water and made for the counter. Patrick held a restraining hand on him. "Hey, I'd kill for a hot shower right now, buddy. Enjoy it."

Dana added some soap and began lathering the puppy. He disliked it intensely, attempting to free himself and shake off the offending soap. "Keep him still!"

"I am! There—that better?" He gained a grip on the soaked dog, which now resembled a drowned rat. Only the eyes and the nose—and the snarls of a canine twice his size—identified the wet lump as dog.

"He must be part toy poodle." Finished with the sudsing, Dana started on the rinse cycle, which the dog liked little better.

"This thing? He's part Tasmanian devil." Patrick used a second hand to restrain the slippery creature.

"Thank you!" She beamed at Patrick, halting in her rinse.

"For what?"

"Assisting. Coming along. Why *are* you here?"

Her face became suffused with color, and Patrick realized she must be remembering what happened at the pool.

"Tomorrow's Friday."

She shot him a bright smile, let the water out of the sink and reached for a washcloth to begin drying the dog. "So it will be. TGIF."

"I meant, it'll be *Friday*."

Her smile faltered. "Friday?"

"Yeah. The asthma reports. I needed to speak to Harrison on board business and I thought I'd stop by to remind you. Have you had a chance to compile the numbers?"

"Oh, crap. No. I mean, sort of. You're not going to like them." She nodded toward her computer as she briskly rubbed down the dog. "Lissa's been helping me keep up."

"Why won't I like the numbers?"

Patrick had let his hold on the dog slacken, and now the little guy broke free and scrabbled out of the sink. Dana grabbed for him, but the dog was like a bullet. He jumped to the floor and darted for cover, but didn't find any.

"This dog!" Patrick stretched out a long arm to corral the little fellow. Back on the counter, the dog stuck his stubby little tail down and set to whimpering once again.

"He's just scared. You have to give him time." Dana pulled back fur on a long cut on the dog's chest. "Shh. Shh. This won't hurt. Much. Here. Keep him over the sink."

If the dog didn't like soap and water, he despised Betadine. Patrick held him as tightly as he dared. "What's wrong with the numbers?"

"There's an uptick." Dana didn't look up from her work as she said this. Her fingers were no less efficient at patching up a dog than they were at patching up a kid. "Okay. He's good."

"So what do I do?" Patrick asked. "I'm afraid to let the rascal go."

"Rascal! That's a good name for him."

"Uh, if you're going to keep him. Are you?"

Dana stared into the puppy's eyes. "I'm not supposed to," she crooned. "But you're too cute to go to the pound."

"Why do I think you'd still say that if this dog was even uglier than he is?"

She gave Patrick a sharp look. "You mean you'd take a dog that we worked so hard to save to the *pound?*"

Patrick squirmed under her scrutiny. "No. Of course not. Not the pound. What do you figure caused the uptick?"

"Maybe I *will* keep him. Kate would like him. And he'd be company." Dana patted Rascal on the head, then pivoted to open a storage closet. The dull rattle of cardboard told Patrick she was finding a box for the puppy. Sure enough, she pulled out a carton. "There. That seems about right."

She popped Rascal into his new home and placed him on the floor. As soon as she did so, the dog turned over the box and dashed for safety in a corner.

"Oh, leave him for now," Dana instructed. "That's probably where he feels safe. Besides, you wanted the asthma reports." She sat down at her computer and began clicking away at the keys.

Why *was* he here? He could have just as easily handled all his school errands via e-mail. The shape his clothes were in from the dog rescue, he'd have to put off talking to Harrison anyway.

"How much of an increase, and what do you feel caused it?" he prompted, evading her question.

"Any number of things, including the one you're worried about."

"The mold? Is it getting worse?"

Dana finished up, and the laser printer beside her whirred to life. She retrieved the papers and handed them to him. "Patrick, I couldn't say. All I do is tally the numbers, and I've warned you that they won't tell the whole story, not without good baseline figures from the students' primary care doctors. But if you want to rule out the possibility you're most concerned about, then properly abate the mold."

His expression darkened. "We can't afford that and you know it."

The puppy nosed out of the corner and sniffed of Patrick's sodden pants leg. Long toenails clicked on the tile floor.

"I don't know it," she protested. "You said yourself

at that meeting that the parents hadn't had a chance to vote. They may not mind a tax increase."

"I've tried. Okay?" The puppy jumped at the sharpness in Patrick's tone and edged closer to Dana, then plopped by her feet.

"You've got a friend for life," Patrick said, attempting to bridge the chasm his words had created.

Dana's mouth tightened. "Don't change the subject."

"Some things are just hopeless, okay? You do the best you can, but you still can't change how they turn out."

"I don't understand you. The school system has a problem, yes, a big one, but surely it's not hopeless." Dana reached down to lift up Rascal. The dog didn't seem to mind her touch. "Have you always been a glass-half-empty kind of guy?"

Patrick pondered her question while he watched her stroke Rascal's fur. The question was a good one, and it highlighted the differences in their perspectives. Her crusading soul exhausted him. Where did she find the energy to rescue the world?

"Maybe. I don't know." Which was a prevarication, because he *did* know. He hadn't always been this way. He just hadn't minded being the person he was until Dana had pointed his pessimism out.

Patrick toyed with the papers in his hands, tapping them against his damp blue jeans, musing. "Are you going to be at the pool tonight?"

"Tonight?" Her fingers slowed as they scratched Rascal behind the ear. The dog snuffled against her hand as if to encourage her to start up again.

"You don't have to avoid the pool on my account."

She fiddled with the computer keyboard, closing out

windows to reveal a screen saver of Kate. "Not sure I was welcome."

Patrick frowned. "You've forgone swimming because of me?"

"I meant what I said about doing no harm."

"You're not." To cover his uncertainty, Patrick flipped back through the pages in his hand, this time more deliberately. "This uptick couldn't be due to the time of the year—colds or something?"

"Of course it could." Rascal gave up on having Dana's undivided attention and leaped off her lap. Dana crossed her legs and propped an elbow on her desk. "Season probably does play a part. It's winter, the prime time for bronchial patients to have difficulties. You don't have pneumonia in the summer."

Patrick rolled the papers back up. He wanted to throw them in the trash but resisted the impulse. "So it is the time of the year."

She stood and moved to begin cleaning up from their dog grooming. "I can't say that. I can't provide you with a blanket assurance that the mold in the lunchroom isn't causing any more problems. And I can't say that it is." Dana banged a door harder than she should have, and it popped back open. She sighed. With gentler fingers, she closed it. "I *can* tell you that mold is a major environmental trigger for a lot of asthma patients, and that at least these kids' parents should be alerted to its presence. I'm serious, Patrick."

"Serious. You're always serious about this. Where's your famous optimism? Nellie was never this concerned. She just handed out tissue and antihistamine."

Dana looked skyward and shook her head. "Nellie was a bit too cavalier, in my opinion. If that mold gets worse, it could trigger a severe anaphylactic reaction in a student. A kid could wind up on a vent. And all these records I'm keeping—well, let's just put it this way. They'll make an ambulance-chasing attorney very happy. I know. That's what my ex does for a living."

"He was an attorney?" Patrick cocked his head. "You, a nurse, married to a lawyer? Did you help him chase ambulances?"

She compressed her lips and bent down. Was it to avoid meeting Patrick's gaze that she knelt, calling for Rascal to come out of the corner? "Not that it's any of your business, but yes, I was a nurse and he was an attorney. We met in the E.R., and he charmed me into a date over a slip-and-fall patient. Before you say it, let me beat you to the punch. I should have known better, and I do know better now."

Rascal waddled out of his hidey-hole. Instead of going to Dana, he started to chew on a corner of his box. Patrick watched as the dog took on the container. The fact that it was two times bigger than he was didn't seem to faze him. Hmm. Rascal had a thing in common with his new mistress.

"Just curious," Patrick said finally, over the racket Rascal was creating. "Maybe that's where you get your litigious streak."

"I do not have a litigious streak. I have a common sense streak, and my common sense tells me you are cruising for a bruising. No, let me correct that. These *kids* are cruising for a bruising."

"You just said you couldn't tell if the increase in numbers was due to the mold or time of the year," Patrick said.

She rose to her feet and folded her arms across her chest, frowning. "Now who's sounding like a smarmy attorney?"

"How should I know? I didn't have the benefit of being married to an ambulance chaser. Say, is your ex that guy who advertises on television? Martin Wilson III?"

Dana closed her eyes and shuddered. "That would be him. So kind of you to remind me."

Patrick was surprised that Dana would ever be attracted to a man who advertised his legal prowess on television. "He's got a weak chin. Not to mention enough Brylcreem in his hair to lube a school bus."

"He wasn't always like that. Well, the weak chin, yeah, he's always had that. But the Brylcreem hairstyle arrived after bimbo number two, who said it made him look more sophisticated." Dana bit her lip.

The box upended over Rascal with a thud, and the puppy began whimpering. Box—one. Dog—zilch. Patrick leaned over and pulled the impromptu cage off to discover a pathetically grateful dog.

"I'm sorry I pried, and then made light of it." Patrick pushed up from his chair, suddenly very conscious of how clammy his clothes felt. "I'm no better than what I accuse other people of…"

"It's all right. I collect lawyer's jokes. It's my revenge," she said lightly. Still, her knuckles had turned white where she'd laced her fingers together. "Really. I'm a lot happier now that I'm on my own."

He didn't want to uncover any more grief. He knew how that felt. After an awkward silence, he said, "Thanks for the reports."

"If not the interpretation?"

Patrick stopped mid-stride on his way to the door. "Funny, you're the optimist, yet you're the one with the gloom and doom. And I'm the grouchy old pessimist, but I'm praying for the best. Fancy that."

"I'm an optimist in thinking there's gotta be a solution out there."

"Maybe." He didn't wish to debate with her about this any longer. Fortunately, Rascal provided distraction. The clatter of puppy nails sounded on the floor as Patrick neared the door. "Uh, what about the dog?"

"I'm keeping him."

"Yeah. But Harrison. He'll have a duck fit if he finds a puppy in here."

Dana went and scooped up Rascal. "You're too right. But I hate to take the little guy to an empty house."

"What if…" Patrick hesitated. "What if I take him?"

"Huh?"

"Just for the afternoon. Just to dog-sit. I'll keep him with me at the shop. And I can drop him at your place tonight. Or—" He broke off. "Or not."

"Well…I was going…" Dana blushed.

If she says she's going on a date…

"Yeah?"

"Lissa was going to babysit Kate tonight so I could swim."

The dog's snuffling was the only noise for a moment as Patrick understood the import of her confession.

"Well, I can bring him to the pool." A beat passed. He tried to figure out her reaction. "Or not."

Dana rubbed the puppy under his chin, a considering expression on her face. "Okay." She extended Rascal toward Patrick. "I'll see you tonight."

CHAPTER ELEVEN

DANA CLOSED her fingers over the handle of the door leading to the pool, then snatched them back. Through the glass, she spotted a figure cutting through the water. Patrick.

Go? Stay? Heck, maybe she needed a daisy to figure out what she should do. *Instead of reciting "he loves me, he loves me not," I pull petals, reciting, "I should go, I should stay."*

So Patrick was at the pool. Big deal. He'd come to return Rascal. And she was there for a swim, not a date.

Not that she'd go on a date in a swimsuit. Dana yanked up on the neckline of her one-piece, which suddenly felt too low-cut despite its high scoop. Her fingers went for the elastic at the thighs and jerked the legs down. This swimsuit was two seasons old, bought for utility, not looks, and it did little to flatter her figure.

If I stand here much longer, I'll be reduced to eeny-meeny-miny-mo.

With that self-loathing thought, Dana wrapped her fingers around the door handle anew and yanked. The muggy air, laden with chlorine, washed over her. She walked over to the chaise longue and dropped her bag. Rascal scuttled under the chairs to cold-nose her against her bare legs. She reached down and gave him a scratch behind his ears.

Patrick stopped abruptly in mid-lap. "Thought you'd chickened out," he said. "I was beginning to figure you'd devised a way to gift me with a dog."

"Me? No." She shook her head and tried not to consider what she looked like in this swimsuit.

"Maybe we shouldn't have a dog here."

Patrick splashed in the water behind her, the sound lazy and unconcerned. "He's okay. Believe it or not, he knows his manners. Won't piddle anywhere that's not covered in newsprint, and he's definitely clear when he needs out. So. You gonna worry about a dog or are you coming in?"

Dana kicked off her shoes. "Yeah. How's the water?"

"Great."

She muffed the dive, but then, how could she concentrate when Patrick hadn't lifted his eyes from her when she'd stood on the board? Once she hit the warm water, she felt she had on an extra layer of clothing.

Maybe that's one of the reasons skinny dippers skinny-dipped. The water felt like a blanket.

Her sense of relief took a hit, though, when Patrick swam over toward her. Dana had expected the evening to go something like the last one, where they'd shared the pool with barely any interaction.

Obviously, Patrick had other ideas.

She swallowed and treaded water, resisting the urge to swim away from him. If he could act cool and calm, then so could she.

He is *cool and calm. He's not simply acting that way.*

Dana jerked as Patrick reached out and slid a fingertip along her face.

At her response, Patrick drew back. "Sorry. Your hair—a strand of it is out of your cap."

"Oh." She tucked the strand back in. "Thanks."

"I'm glad you came tonight."

"Thanks for puppy-sitting Rascal," she said.

Patrick was entirely too close. She drifted from him to get some space, but the wall of the pool thudded against her back. Just as she was about to ask if Rascal had been any further trouble, Patrick asked a question of his own.

"How long?"

How long what? Since her heart had beat double time? Since she'd been alone with a guy she was this aware of?

She repeated his question, as much to buy time as to understand it.

A dimple in Patrick's cheek jumped as he smiled. "You're right. It can mean a bunch of things, and I guess I'm wondering about a lot of them. I meant how long since you swam regularly?"

"A while," Dana admitted. "Can't you tell? I'm rusty."

"Rusty? I certainly wouldn't have wanted to compete against you when you weren't."

She swallowed her hesitation. "What about you? You look like you're at the top of your game."

Patrick shrugged and pushed his hand through the water. The ripples floated out and lapped against Dana's skin.

"Sometimes this pool is the only thing that keeps me sane." He'd uttered the words so softly that Dana almost didn't hear them. She held her breath, not sure what to say to his oblique reference to Annabelle's loss.

In the silence that followed, broken only by the noise from the filter and the sounds of Rascal's explorations, Patrick gazed up expectantly from the water. "Running a business, handling the school board—balancing the two can get a little crazy."

Dana cleared her throat. "Yeah. I can imagine. I don't know how you stand the school board duties. Someone has to do it, but I have to admit, I'm glad it's not me."

"I figured you're the type to relish the challenge."

"What type?" Rascal edged close to her back, sniffing at her neck. His curiosity apparently satisfied, he wandered off again.

"Yeah," Patrick said. He raised his eyebrows in a gesture reminiscent of the last smug guy she'd dated, that "Isn't she so cute when she's all worked up?" look. "You know. The crusading type. Determined to solve all the world's problems with a single bound."

The comment stung, and she had to remind herself that this was the same man who'd gotten down in the muck to help her rescue a dog. She whipped around and started swimming toward the end of the pool. Away from Patrick. Away from this confusing, confounding man.

"Hey! What did I do?" Patrick called to her.

She ignored him, sucked in a lungful of air and swam on. But as she did her somersault to turn back, Patrick was there. He stayed her with light hands on her arms.

"Whoa," he said. "I offended you."

Dana pasted a bright smile on her lips. "I just thought I'd let you get on with your laps."

"No. Something I said, something I did." Patrick scissor-kicked to stay afloat but did not let go of Dana's arms.

She moved from his hold. "Forget it. Okay?"

Patrick shot her a sharp look. "I'm trying here, Dana. But I'm at a loss about what you want."

You. Her answer echoed through her, but she only said, "Maybe what I want shouldn't have anything to do with it."

"I thought you showing up tonight meant something. Starting over, at least. I know I've got my problems. But I'm not a bad sort. Or so I've been told."

Ah, yes, by every eligible woman in Logan, according to Lissa. "Patrick, you're at a loss? Well, so am I. I mean, each time I see you, I get a different version of Patrick. Who's this one?"

"The new and improved version?"

The flip remark, uttered with a good deal of dimple action, reminded her too much of Marty. "Maybe I don't need the new and improved version."

"Then what do you need?"

Somebody who will stand by me. Somebody who doesn't change minute by minute, giving me what he thinks I want. Somebody who isn't a chameleon, giving everybody *what he thinks they want.*

But Dana didn't say that. She didn't say anything. She held back hot tears, shocked that she could still feel so betrayed by Marty after all these years.

"What is it? You're about to cry." Now Patrick's left hand cupped her chin. "I did offend you."

Humiliated by the emotion that swamped her, she attempted to wrench away. Patrick wouldn't let her. His other hand wrapped around her waist and he drew her close. "No. You know about Annabelle. So you tell me. What's this?"

She felt his perfect body against her. To believe he could be everything she wanted, everything she needed, would be so easy. She could fool herself, lie to herself.

But wasn't that what she had done with Marty?

"Patrick. We shouldn't."

"Shouldn't what?" Then he bent down and kissed her.

She should have resisted. She should have broken the kiss.

But this was more than a kiss, more than his lips against hers, more than the mingling of breath and tongues. The sweetness of it had her melting against him, clinging to him.

When she finally found enough sense to pull back, she stretched a trembling hand out to the end of the pool.

"We shouldn't do that," she said. "Definitely not that."

CHAPTER TWELVE

WITH RUBBERY ARMS, Dana hoisted herself up on the rough concrete apron of the pool. Patrick joined her as water sluiced off her, and she realized that the thin wet fabric of her swimsuit was revealing her reaction to him. She turned sideways so he couldn't see the effect he had on her.

The silence between them grew, mostly because Dana couldn't figure out anything to say.

Patrick frowned. "You look like you regret having come here."

"Maybe. A little. I'm not usually so rash."

"A swim is rash?" He cocked an eyebrow questioningly. "Or is it the kiss with me that was rash?"

Dana folded her arms across her chest and faced him full on. "I think we need to keep our relationship professional. This could get complicated," she said.

"Complicated's okay with me."

Dana laughed, remembering Lissa's tale of the ignored messages on his answering machine—and that her definition of *complicated* was "chicken." Well, yes. She was chicken. "Why don't I believe that? Besides, now's just not a good time for me."

"Why don't I believe *that?*" Patrick kicked his feet in the water, sending up a splash.

"Okay. I don't do complicated. I have to keep things simple. I have to focus right now."

Patrick reached over and patted Rascal. The puppy appeared a half size bigger. She saw that Patrick—or someone—had scrounged up a collar for him.

"You still in love with your ex?" Patrick wasn't looking at her as he said the words, and the tone of the question was conversational.

"*No.*"

Patrick surveyed her, then went back to petting the dog. When Rascal scampered off to chase something, Patrick still didn't look at her. Again, he kicked the water. "The ink must be barely dry on the divorce papers, huh?"

That question. She hated that question because it led to calculations about Kate's age and then still more questions.

She pondered how to answer, as Rascal bounced back to her side, his little pink tongue out. Dana decided to circumvent the entire age hassle. "Divorced about three years. Separated since the day Marty found out I was pregnant with Kate."

Patrick stared at her. He worked his mouth, as if trying to frame an appropriate response.

A cell phone buzzed—not hers, but his. Patrick leaped up, so eager to answer it he nearly tripped. He righted himself and retrieved the device from a table.

At first, Dana made an effort not to listen, which was easy enough. All she had to do was focus on the hum of the pool filter and the way Rascal's fur felt under her fingers.

But then she heard Patrick's exasperated, "Lissa! Why didn't you call me sooner?"

Dana scrambled up, leaving Rascal at her feet. "Is something wrong?"

Patrick indicated a no with a violent shake of his head and a roll of his eyes.

"I'm with Dana right now, but I'll come—"

Lissa must have interrupted him, because Patrick's frown grew fiercer and his grip on the phone tightened. He shot a glance at Dana. "No, Lissa, we're not…it's not like that. I was dropping something off. And don't change the subject of your irresponsibility. You should have called earlier. You're just lucky that I was close by. I'll be there in fifteen."

He folded the phone shut. "I've got to go. Lissa's car won't crank."

"She's in her car? She's supposed to be at my place watching—"

"She's at your house. It just occurred to her—" this he uttered with heavy sarcasm "—that it might be a good idea to get the car checked."

Dana pushed aside the stack of towels and sank onto the chaise longue near the table. Her adrenaline rush of fear faded into a dull buzz of relief. "Oh. I was worried…"

Patrick swung up a duffel bag. "I need to go. Her stepfather—" his voice hardened "—wouldn't know a Phillips screwdriver from a flat-head, and Luke, Mel's husband, is on duty tonight. Lissa could have gotten stranded somewhere. She just doesn't think. God. I can't ever remember being that young and that scatterbrained, but I guess I was."

He started off for the change rooms, then pulled up short. "Look, about what you said. Maybe you're right. Maybe we should keep things professional."

And then he was out the door, letting it close behind him dully.

PATRICK HESITATED after he put his truck into park. He gazed at Dana's darkened house into the unforgiving glare of the truck's headlamps. The shutters sagged as if they were weary. The front porch tilted to one side. The whole place could do with another coat of paint, something better than the cheap whitewash Mrs. Ellis, the landlord, slapped on it every five years or so.

Yet somehow, for all this place's faults, to Dana it must have been better than what she'd left behind.

In the light of the tacked-on carport, Patrick spotted Lissa's rattletrap subcompact in the driveway, and Dana's Pacifica sliding past it. He watched Dana get out, retrieve something—the dog—then make her way up the back steps, keys in hand. She paused, waved for him to come in.

Inside? With Kate?

You're a wuss, Connor. A three-year-old completely unglues you.

The scolding served to get him in motion. He switched off the engine and crossed the dimly lit yard to the back door. If this was another one of Lissa's stunts… She'd sounded positively ecstatic at finding him with Dana.

The soles of his work boots ground against the steps as he held on to a rickety rail that required tightening. Dana lived here and was worried about mold in the schools? This place was a deathtrap for a woman with a kid. Lead paint, substandard wiring, loose railings— God knows how many other hazards lurked.

Patrick reached the top step. "I'll just wait out here for Lissa. No need to get your floors dirty with my boots." He tapped one foot against the other and prayed she didn't see through him.

"I was hoping you'd help me with the dog." Dana

lifted Rascal. "I wanted to surprise Kate. Can you wait with him in the kitchen?"

When Patrick couldn't answer, something in her eyes died. "Forget it. It was a stupid idea."

"No. I'll do it," he blurted. "Here. Give him to me."

Patrick found the kitchen deserted but noted telltale signs of Lissa's recent occupation. A bag of her favorite chips, a half-empty bottle of Diet Coke and her iPod lay alongside a stack of textbooks on the table.

Voices, Dana's and Lissa's, filtered to him from some other part of the house as Patrick waited in the kitchen, holding the dog, feeling Rascal shift nervously in his arms.

Then Rascal yipped, and a pitter-patter of feet gunned for him. The sound was unmistakable—the rubber soles of footed jammies. Patrick inhaled sharply.

The footsteps slowed. Two blue eyes peeped around the corner of the door.

"Is that a doggie?" Recognition had apparently banished Kate's shyness. She barreled toward Patrick. "It is!"

Patrick reached out for support as pain ripped through him at the sight of her. Rascal wiggled free and started barking in earnest now.

"Is he mine? Did you bring him to me? Mommy! Can I keep him?" She was on the floor now with Rascal, who was backing away from this strange creature. "Oh. He doesn't like me."

"No, no, sugar, he's just scared." Patrick squatted on the floor beside her and drew the puppy gentle. "Easy. That's it, nice and slow. Let him get to know you."

Kate put out a plump little hand, then peered up at Patrick for reassurance. He nodded. "Go ahead."

Her eyes rounded in amazement as she petted the

dog. Emboldened, Kate crawled into Patrick's lap beside the dog. Patrick held his breath.

"Well, seems my surprise is out of the bag," Dana burbled with amusement.

"Can I keep him, Mommy? Is he mine?"

For a crazy moment, Patrick was jealous of the dog. He wanted to belong to this family. But that was ridiculous.

"I didn't know you were coming, Mr. Patrick." Kate bestowed on him the full measure of her charm, batting her eyelashes like only a three-year-old princess could. His heart turned.

"Neither did I, but here I am."

Something about what he'd said made Kate giggle.

"Mr. Patrick helped save your puppy," Dana explained. "You'd better thank him."

If this child thanked him, he would fall apart. "His name is Rascal," Patrick told Kate quickly.

"And you saved him? Was he hurt?"

"Yes. He has a cut. Your mom put medicine on him."

"My mommy's good at fixing things."

Patrick swallowed. He had to get out of there before he fell into the trap of thinking that life could ever be normal.

Lissa's cell phone rang with some raucous song that resembled metal being dragged across pavement. She yanked the phone to her ear with a greeting. An instant later, her jaw had set and her mouth had turned down.

"Yes, I called him, Mel. My car was slow to start. No! That is not it!" Lissa eyed her father, her frown deepening. She pivoted and spoke in a lower but still furious, tone.

Patrick couldn't make out the words. Yet he didn't have to. He recognized the bickering between his daughters. He checked on Kate, who was still focused on the puppy and seemingly oblivious to the telephone quarrel.

Lissa's voice grew harder and colder. "Fine. Call me selfish. That's what you do anyway." And she hung up. She faced them all with a fake bright smile, as though the argument hadn't happened. "Looks like you've made a new friend, Dad."

As Lissa started to answer, Patrick's phone rang. He went for the clip on his belt, and Kate wriggled off his lap to play with Rascal.

"Mommy! Can Rascal sleep in my room tonight? Can he?"

By now, Patrick had the phone open. Melanie was on the other end.

"Dad, I am so sorry. I don't know *what* Lissa was thinking, asking you to go *there*— What's that racket?"

Patrick glanced at the floor, where Rascal was yipping joyously as Kate pursued him. Lissa, from the glower on her face, had guessed who the caller was. "It's a puppy, Mel. It's okay," he lied. "Dana and I were just finishing up with laps and so I followed Dana home. I'll listen to Lissa's engine and see what the problem is."

"There *is* no problem. Mark my words. That car is fine, Dad," Mel said. "She's just determined to make you miserable, or else she's trying to prove that she *needs* a new car."

Dana was on the floor now, joining in the fray. Patrick longed to be as carefree as she was. He knew, watching Dana with Kate and Rascal, that her love was the fearless kind. She could still love freely, without holding anything back. He missed that. Why couldn't it be that simple for him?

"Dad?" Mel prompted. "Did I lose you? You still there?"

Then, as if the chaos of babysitting, sibling rivalry, car trouble and a puppy weren't enough, Kate sucker punched Patrick with a tight embrace around his knees. "I love you, Mr. Patrick! Thank you for the puppy!"

CHAPTER THIRTEEN

THROUGH THE PHONE, Mel's breath made a hissing sound as she inhaled. "You got her a puppy?"

"Mel." Patrick yanked himself back to the present and put as much loving firmness into her name as he could to stop her. "It's okay. He's a stray. Dana found him. Don't make such a big deal out of it."

Patrick said goodbye to an unconvinced Mel and closed the phone. He could not prevent his other hand from touching Kate's curls.

She gazed up at him, so like Annabelle, yet so different. "Hey, punchinello," he said, wincing as he heard himself use the nickname he'd had for Annabelle. "It's late. Shouldn't you be snug in bed?"

"With Rascal. Rascal's gonna sleep with me tonight."

Dana let out an exaggerated sigh. "I doubt anybody in this house will get any sleep. But we should be heading to the bed."

Kate pirouetted away from Patrick and back to Rascal. Coming here had been a mistake. He was going to lose it. He couldn't. He couldn't let Dana and Lissa realize how raw his emotions were after all these years.

Get a grip, Connor. Deal with your feelings later. What good will crying do?

His speech, familiar to him from the many times he'd had to give it to himself over the years, steadied him.

"Patrick?"

Dana's prompt jolted him. He lifted his head to find her eyeing him quizzically. Glancing down, he saw that Kate was holding the puppy in her arms, a joyful, triumphant, master-of-the-universe smile on her lips.

Annabelle. I miss you.

"Are you okay?" Dana asked.

He rubbed at his eyes and nodded. "Yeah, sure. I'm fine. Why wouldn't I be?"

And then he bolted the hell out of there.

DANA PLACED the adjustable wrench back in her toolbox and returned the box to her broom closet. "So you've got Lissa's car working again?" she inquired, more to banish the silence than to confirm something she already knew.

Patrick stood in her kitchen again, his face drawn. "For now, anyway. A bad battery cable end. She'll have to get a new one, but it will get her home tonight."

"Good." The word dropped into a long silence. Dana didn't know what to say and Patrick appeared to not even be aware of how quiet it was.

Dana cleared her throat. "Can I make you a cup of coffee?"

It took Patrick a moment for to shake his head. "Thanks, no. I'll be heading off."

But he made no move to leave. Instead, he remained where he was by the sink, a frown of concentration on his face. It was as though his thoughts were so deep that they consumed all his energy.

A few moments of holding Kate. That was all it had

taken to turn him into this preoccupied man—transfixed, presumably—anyway, by memories of his own daughter.

Dana's heart ached for him. Her common sense, though, held up Patrick's demeanor as proof positive that indeed he didn't do complicated.

No. Patrick *couldn't* do complicated.

He sagged with fatigue and sighed. Extending a hand, he traced the fabric of Dana's sleeve. Then he met her eyes, and she saw a resignation in his.

He dropped his hand to his side. "I could have a great time with a woman like you, Dana. Tonight—well, tonight was evidence of that."

"But?"

Why did she have to ask? She didn't, not really. Dana waited, the hum of the fluorescent light above the sink especially loud in the silence, for the answer she knew was coming.

"Annabelle." His reply was so soft that she was half-convinced he hadn't uttered it at all.

She didn't get the chance to make certain. Patrick spun on his heel and was out the back door, letting it close behind him with a thud.

AFTER A SLEEPLESS NIGHT filled with nightmares of Kate getting hurt or sick or lost, Dana struggled to face the day's work. Suze shot her a wicked smile as Dana punched in scant minutes before being late.

"Big night, huh? Lissa told me that she was watching Kate so you could go swimming…but I understand *Patrick* showed up." Suze followed her to the clinic door, where Dana paused, trying to figure out which key was the right one and why she was having so much difficulty with such a simple task. "Lissa stopped by, but when she saw you weren't in yet, she said to tell you she was going to grab a cappuccino at the convenience store."

Dana covered a yawn. Coffee sounded like an excellent idea. "It was a late night, that's for certain. But not because of Patrick. Well, yeah, maybe Patrick."

The lock turned and Dana pushed open the door.

"Uh-huh? So which is it? Patrick or not Patrick?" Suze was on her heels.

"More like Lissa and a bum battery. And ghosts." She started the morning's prep with an eye for her first customer and recapped the night's events.

"Oh, honey. I'm sorry." Suze collapsed into the plastic chair beside Dana's desk. "I thought, from what Lissa had said, that you and Patrick might... I don't know, make a go of it. He's sure due something. And perhaps if he could find it, he could forgive my sister."

Dana's eyelids stung, maybe from lack of sleep, maybe from tears. She busied herself with her clipboard and its checklist of students. "It's okay. I don't need the complication at this point. I guess what got me was how *stuck* he looked. It was as though he wanted to move forward, but he couldn't figure out how."

"That's Patrick. That's how Patrick's been for all these years." Suze fiddled with her school ID, which hung from a lanyard. After a beat or two, she said, "Jenny's a little concerned."

"His ex-wife, Jenny?" Dana did a doubletake to make certain Suze was serious, nearly dropping her stack of paper dose cups in the process. "About what?"

"You. Patrick. The girls."

Dana blinked. "What? You've been talking about me to Jenny? Why does this feel so weird?"

"She *is* my sister. And the mother of Patrick's

daughters. She's not a witch, you know. She genuinely cares for him."

With fingers that trembled more than she wished to admit, Dana set down the dose cups and began sorting morning meds. "Okay, so she cares. But I still don't get her interest in me. Does she vet all Patrick's dates?"

"In a town this size?" Suze chuckled. "She doesn't have to."

"I see. If I were a hometown girl, she wouldn't have to interview me." Dana yanked open the fridge and checked the meds inside. Yep, all there, present and accounted for. "Honestly, Suze, last night proves she doesn't have to be concerned at all. I'm the last person Patrick is going to date. I know that. He knows that."

Suze beat out a rat-a-tat-tat on the counter. "She's worried because of the friction created between Mel and Lissa."

"Well, you can tell her—" Dana squeezed her eyes shut and struggled to put her frazzled thoughts in order "—I'm not here to cause trouble, okay? I have no idea what Lissa has said, but as I pointed out, Patrick's stuck. He as much as told me that yesterday evening. And the last person I need to get involved with is a man who can't handle children."

CHAPTER FOURTEEN

PATRICK GRIPPED the school lunchroom tray. Behind the counter, lunchroom worker Lanie Jeffers presided over steaming trays of some sort of turkey version of salisbury steak. "Want more, Mr. Connor?" she asked, apparently in response to the way he hadn't moved on.

He jerked his attention from Dana's blond hair, which was unmistakable because she towered over the rest of the students and staff in the serving line.

Now Patrick managed a smile across the serving line. "Oh, no, Mrs. Jeffers. This is enough." More than enough, since he wasn't so sure what it would taste like.

As Patrick moved along the line to the section with glasses of iced tea, he felt a hand come down on his shoulder. From the hand's weight and size, it could belong to no one other than Vann Hobbes.

"Patrick, sorry I'm late. Got your lunch? Great!" Patrick's best friend wore his "school superintendent casual" attire, as Patrick had dubbed it—pullover sweater, button-down shirt and simple tie. A glance at the tie's knot revealed a flock of roadrunners. Just like Vann to look the superintendent part except on closer inspection.

"No problem," he told Vann, grabbing up a glass of iced tea. He gazed past Vann's shoulder to see Dana moving into the lunchroom proper.

Vann didn't notice Patrick's shifting attention, apparently, as he took the tray Mrs. Jeffers offered. The tray passed by Patrick, and he noted the extra helping of the turkey and the gravy dish. Maybe the meal wouldn't be so bad after all. Or maybe what Lissa and Mel said was true. Vann's appetite was legendary; he'd eat almost anything.

Patrick trailed after Vann as he strode into the cafeteria. He suddenly stopped in front of Patrick, and Patrick suppressed a groan as his friend yanked him to the right, toward Dana and Suze, who were at a small round table next to the longer tables for the kids. "There's a seat with Suze and that new nurse. Let's sit with them."

Let's not.

But how could he avoid it now that Vann had already settled his big frame on the narrow chair beside Suze? Which left him with nowhere to sit except beside Dana.

Dana glanced up from a salad she was pouring dressing over. "Oh. Hi, Patrick." Her surprise showed.

Well, why wouldn't it? He'd been the one who'd bailed from her kitchen as though it had been on fire.

Her gaze traveled to Vann, who was already in animated conversation with Suze, then back to Patrick. "Have a seat," she offered, and he knew she'd grasped that the idea to sit there hadn't been his.

"Thanks." He pulled out the chair and sat down, then he poked at the turkey version of salisbury steak.

"It's not bad," Dana murmured.

"Right. So why are you eating the salad if this is so great?"

Scintillating conversation, Connor. Your small talk is brilliant.

Dana shrugged. "Felt like eating my leafy greens today."

The awkwardness between them kept him silent as he sampled the turkey. Not bad. Not great, either. But for two bucks and a quarter, what could you expect?

Patrick suppressed the urge to glower at Vann. Why did he want Patrick there if Vann intended to spend the whole time talking with Suze? His friend was a good soul, could run a school system like nobody's business. But where social sensitivity was concerned—say, not sitting beside Patrick's ex-sister-in-law—Vann was a little thick.

It's not Suze who bothers you.

"So." The one who really bothered him cleared her throat. "I hear you've already fixed Lissa's car with more than just a temporary patch."

"Yeah."

In response to his monosyllabic answer, Dana hesitated for a second, then grabbed a napkin out of the dispenser in the center of the table. Her jerky movements as she shook the napkin out shouted her annoyance.

Patrick pushed around the turkey on his plate. *Terrific work, Connor.*

He gave conversation another try. "I fixed her battery cable."

Dana's expression lightened. "So it was a bad end?"

"Yeah. Not letting the car get enough juice, draining the battery. Nothing to it to fix it. Anytime you're in need of a jolt or two, I'm your man."

No sooner were the words out of his mouth than Patrick wanted to crawl under the table. His instant embarrassment at the unwitting double entendre was compounded when he realized he'd uttered it in a lull of conversation between Suze and Vann. They stared at him, wide-eyed.

"Lissa's battery. It's a long story. You had to be

there." Patrick dropped his fork, intent on relinquishing any pretense of eating lunch. He couldn't think when this woman was around, much less do more mundane things like eat.

But before he could push back his chair, Dana's chuckle stopped him. His reward for taking another stab at conversation? He couldn't be certain. But the sound of her laughter was great. It wasn't her best laugh, the rich and throaty one that made you want to join in, too, even if you didn't know what was funny. Still, it was a laugh, and he'd take that any day.

Vann recovered first. "Maybe it's good I wasn't there."

Dana answered. "Patrick helped me save a puppy yesterday—and deliver it to Kate."

Vann paused, fork halfway to his mouth. "Huh? I haven't heard about this."

Patrick just shrugged. "It was a stray. The varmint's so ugly he's cute. So Vann, what's new around here?"

Vann's eyes lost their twinkle. He pushed away his tray, now emptied of everything including the beets.

"I was going to wait until later, but now is just as good. We've got some parents expressing concern about the mold. In response to that newspaper coverage of the meeting."

The small amount of turkey and gravy Patrick had been able to consume congealed into a brick in his stomach. He realized that he'd been so focused on Dana that, for the first time, he'd sat in this lunchroom without worrying about whether they'd gotten rid of all the mold. "What…level of concern?"

"You know parents." Vann spread his hands. "It started off with one, whom I thought I had soothed. Then she went away and got another one stirred up, and then the two of them managed to stir up two more, and so on."

"Because of what I said?" Dana asked.

"Because of the story. Beyond that, I couldn't say. Except for the first parent involved, it's a little weird, because the parents who complained don't have kids we test—I mean, *you* test, Ms. Wilson. They're new ones. I was going to talk to you, anyway, about adding them to our testing roster. And I wanted to check."

"Check?" Dana frowned.

"To see if they'd been in your clinic complaining of allergy symptoms. Or, let's see." Vann stuck one giant hand down the neck of his sweater and extracted a slip of paper from his shirt pocket. "Headaches. Nosebleeds. Fatigue."

Vann laid the paper on the table and smoothed it out with enough care to belie his casual attitude. "Is it possible, Ms. Wilson?"

"What?" she croaked.

"That the residual mold could cause problems like this in the general population?"

Dana didn't answer for a long moment. Patrick watched as she mutilated a piece of lettuce on her plate.

"Ms. Wilson?"

Vann was speaking in his whiplike "superintendent" tone, as pointed as any lawyer's cross-examination.

"It's…possible." The lettuce now macerated, she slid over her fork to attack a radish. "It would signal a much higher level of mold than you've indicated you were dealing with."

Patrick's stomach took another hit. That turkey was wreaking havoc on him. He attempted to settle his nerves by sipping his iced tea. "How so?"

"Well." Dana screwed up her features in concentration. "The reason people get in trouble with mold to begin with is that it provokes an autoimmune response.

At high enough levels, mold can cause a reaction even in people who haven't formerly shown allergies."

"That doesn't sound so good." Vann traded a look with Patrick. "Did you know this? Ms. Wilson, do you mean we could be creating allergies—"

"Yeah, that's exactly what I mean," Dana said. "The kicker is, once a person has an allergic response, even a mild one, from then on the body interprets the causative substance as foreign. It then scrambles an autoimmune response to attack the substance, and it gets better and better at it each time. Which is worse for the patient."

"Like bee stings?" Suze asked. "My son's pediatrician told us that based on my son's reaction to a sting when he was little, we should avoid bees like the plague and keep an EpiPen handy. But the reaction didn't look huge to me at the time. I'm not doubting the doctor— I keep EpiPens everywhere."

Dana nodded. "Yeah. The first sting wasn't fatal because your son's body wasn't geared up for it. But next time, without intervention a bee sting could produce a much more severe reaction."

"Again with the anaphylactic shock business?" Patrick rolled his eyes. "I did a whale of a lot of research, and I never saw that."

Dana wheeled to face him with a scowl. "A reaction that extreme is rare, granted, but you could well be creating sensitivities with the mold. A person who never had problems with mold allergies could, day after day, build up a sensitivity to it. Hey." She threw up her hands. "Mr. Hobbes asked."

Vann looked as though he had more questions. Patrick cut him off. "Who is the one parent? The one you said that if not for her, this would be weird."

"Oh. You're gonna love this." Vann leaned back in his chair. "Mrs. Lawsuit herself."

"You've got to be kidding. You had me all worried over her?" Patrick leaned back, as well, his hands easing out of the fists he hadn't even realized they'd formed.

"Who?" Dana asked.

"Tammy Mayhew," Suze supplied. "She's always going to the board with some wild complaint, swearing that if the board doesn't fix whatever the ailment du jour is, she'll sue."

"Oh, Lord." Dana's face went a shade paler.

"Relax," Patrick told her. "No biggie. The woman has the attention span of a gnat. Plus she has three kids, one in each of our schools, so she's always outraged about something. She never gets around to actually filing a suit or even contacting an attorney. She's too busy getting outraged by the next 'big problem.'" He used his fingers again to signal quotes around *big problem*.

Dana remained tense. "I wouldn't discount her so quickly."

"You're thinking like your litigious ex-husband." He turned to the others. "Were you aware she was married to Mr. Martin Wilson III?"

"No kidding. The guy on TV? The 'You can sue, I can help' guy?" Vann inquired. "You married him? Is he as irritating in real life as he is on television?"

"He had his moments," Dana muttered. She shot Patrick a look of equal parts betrayal and embarrassment. "But yes, I learned a lot from him about why people sue."

Patrick snorted. "That's easy. People sue because they think they can get money out of deep pockets."

"Not always," Dana protested. "Maybe in the end. But in the beginning? They want the defendant to accept responsibility for something huge that has happened in their lives. And if this woman has threatened in the past, she may just not have found a lawyer yet who was willing to take her on. But this…"

"What's so different about this?" Patrick queried.

"Well, for one thing, she's got a scientific leg to stand on. And for another…" Dana crumpled her napkin and tossed it atop the small hillock of leafy greens still left on her plate. "She's got legal precedent on her side."

CHAPTER FIFTEEN

THE FINAL LUNCH BELL rang, interrupting their impromptu meeting. Despite the spin her thoughts were
in, Dana found herself responding to the bell with Pav-
lovian predictability. She pushed her chair back and
grabbed her plate ready to race back to work. She noted
with some amusement that neither the superintendent
nor Patrick seemed the slightest bit rushed, whereas
Suze followed her lead.

"Mr. Hobbes, Patrick. If you have any more questions,
I'll be in the clinic. I have after-lunch meds to adminis-
ter."

Dana headed for the trash cans and the plate drop-
off, not waiting to hear if they had more questions for
her. She needed time to think. They obviously didn't
feel this new group of students was a real problem, but
Dana sensed it was.

*And you created this mess by going to the board,
getting the problem in the papers.*

No, wait. That wasn't entirely fair. She flashed back
to Patrick, who'd told her to show up to begin with. He
of all people should have known the press would be
there, and that her concerns would ignite the more litigious folks in town.

*He was bluffing, and you called him on it. He didn't
believe you'd show up.*

Dana raked the scraps on her plate into the trash with more force than she'd intended. The lunchroom ladies behind the drop-off bay gave her a startled look.

"Bad day?" one of them asked.

Dana glanced over her shoulder at Patrick, who was still sitting with Vann Hobbes. "You have no idea."

Behind her Suze tip-tapped in her high heels. "Got a minute to talk before your first patient?"

"If you don't mind walking with me to the clinic," Dana told her.

"Actually, that'd be better anyway." Now Suze's eyes traveled back toward the table she and Dana had just left.

"Uh-oh. Somehow I'm not getting a good feel about this."

"It's not bad. Well, I don't believe so, anyhow."

They left the lunchroom and were halfway down the hall before Suze spoke again. "Jenny's stopping by to chat with you."

"What?" Dana squeaked. "With Patrick in the same building? Most likely coming to my clinic?"

"Forgive me for poor timing. I had no idea that Patrick would drop in for lunch with you today. You should have told me."

"Oh, right, like he wanted to be within a hundred miles of me." Dana rolled her eyes. "You saw him. He was with Hobbes, *not* me."

"Can you slow down?" Suze's heels tapped faster on the highly polished tile as she struggled to keep up with Dana's agitated stride.

"Can I help it if my legs are twice as long as yours?" But Dana did decrease her pace.

Suze caught up with her. "This isn't about Patrick. This is about Lissa and Mel."

Dana halted. "Suze, one is interning with me, and the other I barely know."

"Put yourself in Jen's shoes, Dana. Her daughters are in a bitter disagreement over whether their dad should be dating—"

"We will not be dating, not if I have any sense at all," Dana said firmly. "The man is carrying enough baggage for ten people on a year-long trip to Europe. He's not ready to be a father, and I'd be a fool to get involved with another man like that. I need to stop this day-dreaming about what life could be like with Patrick if he got unstuck and if he suddenly developed a non-bean-counter heart."

A rich laugh came from behind her. "Good luck, then. Because none of that is about to happen."

Dana turned to see a woman standing in a doorway, a woman who could only be Patrick's Jenny.

VANN HAD CADGED another piece of cake from the lunchroom ladies and was attacking it with gusto. Patrick watched him, wondering when Vann would surface for air and tackle him about Dana. One thing about the man—he might appear fully absorbed in a task, but he noticed more than he let on. That attribute had been Patrick's savior as a high school quarterback with Vann in his offensive line.

Sure enough, Vann had more on his mind. He forked in the last bite of cake, shoved the saucer away from him, leaned on his elbows and peered at Patrick.

Patrick didn't say anything. If Vann wanted to know something, he'd have to ask, and even then Patrick wasn't sure what he'd tell him.

"So. Dana." That was it. Vann's question, summed up in two words. This would be easy enough to evade.

"She seems on top of things, but with overtones of Chicken Little." Patrick had opted for the professional assessment. Who knows? Maybe that was what Vann had been asking.

"She's got something, though, with the Mayhew woman."

Thankfully, Vann's eyes never settled for more than a second or two on Patrick. Instead, they roved the emptying lunchroom, in one what Patrick joked was his "superintendentator" mode.

Patrick grabbed the chance to steer the conversation away from Dana. "Yeah, well, the Mayhew woman hasn't sued us yet. And I honestly don't feel she has a leg to stand on. Regardless of what Dana says."

So much for distraction and redirection, Connor. It seemed that he couldn't budge from thinking about her.

Vann frowned as he stared out across the lunchroom. For a moment, Patrick thought the frown was in reaction to what he'd said. Then he followed Vann's gaze and saw two fifth-graders tangling in the cafeteria line. Vann relaxed when a teacher arrived and sorted out the squabble. He switched his focus back to Patrick.

"Chicken Little, huh? That all you think of her?"

Crap.

"Of course not. I think she does a good job. She's smart and compassionate with the kids. I'm not questioning your judgment, Vann."

Vann shot him a crooked smile and fiddled with the plastic wrap that had covered the now-history cake. "I understand that. I wasn't asking about whether I made a mistake in hiring her."

"Oh." Now Patrick craved something to do with his hands. He considered nibbling on the turkey disaster still on his plate but couldn't stomach the prospect.

"So? Do I have to spell it out?"

Patrick shook the ice in his glass. Less than a good swallow of tea was in there. Would it be obvious to Vann that he was trying to avoid the subject of Dana by going for a refill?

"Guess I do, buddy. Okay. One—you show up with her for the board meeting at the last minute and have her on the agenda. Two—Lissa is babysitting Dana's little girl. Three—you rescue a puppy and give it to Kate."

Patrick didn't get the chance to protest, because Vann had moved on to point four. "And four—you go all sixth-grade on me when I want to sit with her today."

"I did not go all sixth-grade on you," Patrick retorted. "What the heck does that mean, anyway?"

"Teresa Sikes. Sixth grade. Vegetable soup day. Ring any bells?"

Patrick snorted. "Do you not forget anything? So I spilled vegetable soup all over me that day."

"And me—don't forget me." Vann tapped himself on the chest. "All because when I went right, toward Teresa Sikes's table, you went left, directly into me. Hey. It's been decades. It should be funny now."

"But it's not. You've recovered. You're a school superintendent."

"Which should tell you I'm as crazy as a bedbug and let you know I'm still suffering repercussions," Vann cracked. Then he grew more serious. "Today, I was thanking God I remembered to get in front of you and I didn't have any vegetable soup on my tray. You've gone and pulled the same stunt. Only, this time you are way too old to be running from your grown-up equivalent of Teresa Sikes."

Patrick raised his eyebrows and tried another evasion method. "Wonder where ol' Teresa is these days?"

"Not here. And not Dana."

Vann was simply not going to leave this subject alone, was he? Resigned, Patrick drank the less-than-a-swallow amount of tea in his glass and set the glass down with a thunk. "Okay. She's pretty. She's funny. She's got legs ten miles long. Are you asking permission to go out with her?"

"Not me, buddy. I'm the one who works for the school system. Even if I wanted to, that's verboten."

"Oh." Patrick hoped he hid his relief well. Was he such a dog in the manger that he wouldn't want his friend to date Dana even if he'd decided that he couldn't?

Had he decided that?

Vann still didn't let him off the hook. "You." He leveled a finger at Patrick.

"What?" This was as bad as playing chess with Vann when he had gotten everything but your king, a pawn and one knight. He'd chase you all over the board until he had you hemmed in.

Patrick conceded defeat. "I'm not dating Dana. Lissa tried to set us up, God knows why, which is the reason for the two times we swam together."

"Two? I only heard about one." Vann rubbed his hands. "So you've had two dates with her?"

"No. What part of 'I'm not dating Dana' don't you understand? Vann, she's all the things I said, and yes, probably more, but it's not going to happen."

Vann's attention had wandered to a custodian beginning to mop the far corner of the lunchroom. "Wonder whether we could free up the janitors if we bought a few of those automatic mopping robots—you know, those Scoobas, or whatever they're called."

"We barely have money for new mops, Vann."

"True. Why is it not going to happen?"

"Because those suckers cost, what, three or four—"

"No, not the Scoobas—I was just dreaming is all. Dana. She tell you to get lost?"

"Now who's going all sixth-grade. Dana and I are adults, Vann. We don't have to tell each other to get lost. We look at the situation, see it's got no future and end it before anybody gets hurt. *Before* it starts."

"Mature." Vann's voice dripped with sarcasm.

"And this coming from the man who's had the same batting average with matrimony as me? And who is still not in a committed relationship?" Patrick scoffed. "Right."

Vann stacked up his dishes, then took his last drink of tea, the ice rattling against the inside of the plastic tumbler. He pinned a knowing stare on Patrick. "Let me guess. This has nothing to do with anything current, except maybe Dana's daughter."

Check and checkmate. Patrick attempted to draw in a breath, but his chest had gone tight on him. He couldn't speak, which was just as well, because Vann had continued.

"Patrick, I've been there. With you. I know what a living hell you were in. But there are no good guys and no bad guys. Just human beings, with weaknesses and frailties. And the sooner you get that through your head, the sooner you don't have to end things before they start."

Vann turned and headed for the plate drop-off. Patrick was left alone at the table, the custodian behind him whistling as he mopped up spilled milk.

CHAPTER SIXTEEN

DANA FOUGHT THE URGE to lock the door behind her and Jenny in the clinic. That would prevent Patrick from waltzing in on them. She wasn't doing anything wrong. So why did she feel guilty about talking with Patrick's ex-wife?

You're not even dating him.

Jenny surveyed the little clinic with interest. She sat in the chair Suze usually favored and across from where Dana was seated at her desk. Jenny was the grown-up version of Lissa: blond hair that was silky straight, slim build, the eyes, nose and chin that Lissa had inherited.

Suze had ditched Dana and Jenny, rat that she was, and now Dana found herself stuck, not knowing what to say. What did a woman say to the ex-wife of the guy you wanted to lose your mind with?

The truth—that was what you said. "I'm not sure what you are hoping to accomplish here. I'm not involved with Patrick." There, honest enough.

Jenny laughed, and Dana wanted to hate her for the lovely sound Jenny's laugh made. The package was too perfect, from the Ann Taylor jacket to the kitten heels.

And the hair. She'd kill for hair like that.

Something, though—maybe the way Jenny reminded her of Lissa—made Dana unable to work up any antipathy.

Still smiling, Jenny went on. "You said you needed to stop daydreaming about Patrick. And I said it wasn't going to happen. I have Patrick experience. I know." The laughter in Jenny's eyes faded, and a somberness took its place.

Was Jenny still in love with Patrick? That was even more reason for Dana to stay far, far away from him.

Jenny reached into a bag that would have set Dana back half a week's salary and brought out a leather clutch. She ran her fingers in a zipper compartment inside the wallet and presented Dana with a small wallet-size photo.

Dana hesitated before she accepted the picture. Staring back at her were younger versions of Patrick and Jenny, along with three beautiful little girls. The photographer had caught Patrick chuckling.

Tears pricked at Dana's eyes. The image of a happy little family soon to be destroyed made it as unbearable to view as a movie you knew would end badly. "He looks happy. You all look happy."

"We were. I mean, don't get me wrong. It was a marriage, and no marriage is perfect. But Patrick was a great husband and father. A wonderful man. And generous—to a fault."

Dana handed the picture back to Jenny. She watched as Jenny's fingers trembled while she tucked the picture in its hideaway again. What was her point? To tell Dana to back off?

Now Jenny's voice cracked when she spoke. "It ended. All of it. We might as well have filed for divorce the day we came home from speaking with Annabelle's pediatrician. Patrick couldn't deal with Annabelle being so sick. He could never admit to himself that we were going to lose her. Even on the day she died, he refused to believe the doctors when they told us the end was near."

"And you?"

"Me? I was out of my mind. I couldn't ignore what the doctors said. I couldn't deny what I saw with my own eyes. A mother knows." Jenny's eyes were shiny-bright, but she blinked the tears away. "Once what the doctors were saying sank in, the important thing to me was Annabelle. Keeping her comfortable. Making sure she wasn't scared."

"Yeah. I can understand that."

Jenny steepled her fingers. She sat very still in the chair, as if considering what to say next.

Her decision apparently made, she sighed. "Something else was important, too. I knew I had to care for *all* my girls. Looks like I still do."

Dana pushed her hair, corkscrew curly and so far removed from Jenny's sleek style, off her face. She attempted to gauge the direction of the conversation. "Jenny. I'm honestly not trying to make trouble—"

A small amount of irritation marred Jenny's smooth forehead "But you are, aren't you? Whether or not you mean to."

The comment found its mark. Dana couldn't deny that she was a bone of contention for Mel. Still, Jenny's presence annoyed her. "So what would you have me do?"

"Why'd you give Lissa an internship?"

The sudden change in subject threw Dana for a moment. "Why shouldn't I have? It had nothing to do with Patrick." Well, not much, anyhow, and not in the way Jenny was thinking.

Jenny cleared up the confusion with her next words. "Melanie is completely set against you. She's certain you gave Lissa the internship to curry favor with Patrick. I hate to see the relationship between my daughters suffer another hit. They've already been through a lot, and they were just coming around to each other. I had hoped this would be a chance for them to reconcile."

Dana was struggling to figure out a reply when the door opened wide and revealed Patrick.

"Dana, got a minute? I'd like to—"

He stood stock-still in the doorway, looking first at Dana and then Jenny.

There was no malevolence in his expression. No hostility. Just bewilderment.

And then the bewilderment was replaced with that shuttered expression she now knew so well. He went poker-faced; only his eyes showed sadness, betrayal.

"I guess you don't have a minute." He yanked the door shut behind him.

Dana groaned. "You happy?" she snapped at Jenny before chasing after Patrick.

Out in the hall, she spotted Patrick rounding the corner to an exit. "Patrick!" she called, but he didn't reappear.

She hustled to follow him, past classrooms with children bent over deskwork, past bulletin boards full of prized papers and seasonal scenes.

The outer door opened, and she called out again. "Patrick! Wait up!"

But the only reply was a *clunk* as the door shut. By now Dana had reached the corner. She made the turn in time to see the door clicking into place and, through a small window, Patrick making a bead for the parking lot.

He'd heard her. And ignored her. She ground her teeth in exasperation and followed him outside. This time Dana didn't waste any breath calling after him. She took advantage of his slowed pace to catch up with him at his truck.

"Patrick, I am so sorry. You have to believe me—"

"What do I have to believe?" he snapped.

"I had nothing to do with her being here. Believe me."

"Maybe I can't. She *left,* Dana. Left at the worst possible time and in the worst possible way, and I just cannot write her a blank check of forgiveness. No matter what you or Suze or Vann say. I can't."

Dana was nonplussed at his words. "When I have I asked you to forgive anybody? Except me for getting stuck with her?"

Patrick clenched the door handle of the truck. "Forget it. It's not important. I don't like it when people talk about me behind my back."

Dana thought about how she'd felt when she'd realized she was a topic of conversation for Jenny and her family. "Join the crowd," she muttered. "I'm sorry. Whether you accept it or not, she sought me out, not the other way around. I wasn't having a gossip session with her." Dana didn't need this. She needed the quiet small-town life she'd dreamed about for her and for Kate.

With that thought in mind, she turned away from Patrick and headed back to the building.

CHAPTER SEVENTEEN

PATRICK WATCHED Dana go. Vann's words about starting things came back to him. Everybody, it seemed, honestly thought that he couldn't have a relationship with a woman. He was in a perverse enough mood now to prove them wrong.

If the woman had been anybody but Dana, that is. Who had a child. Why did he let Kate unnerve him?

Dana had reached the grass now, her shoulders bent, her head down. She was power walking on those incredible legs of hers.

"Ah, hell." Patrick let go of the truck door and started after her. He couldn't seem to kick the habit of hurting her feelings, and now he would have to apologize to her one more time. She was right. All they ever did was tell each other they were sorry. "Dana!"

She stopped short, glanced over her shoulder. A light wind kicked up, caught that curly hair of hers and teased it. He had an incredibly irresistible urge to run his fingers through it.

Patrick closed the gap to find her arms crossed against the chill in the air. She'd followed him outside in just her scrubs, no jacket.

"I'm sorry," he said.

"No problem." Her tone was as chilly as the air around them.

"I'd like to say I know what's going on with me at the moment, but I don't. Jenny was the last person I expected to see in your office, and I just flipped out."

Dana regarded him with an unconvinced expression. "This is a pretty small town. How do you avoid her?"

"Usually, we travel in different enough circles that I don't run into her. When something's going on with the girls and I know she'll be there, well, I just psych myself up. These unexpected times are the kicker."

Now Dana cocked her head with curiosity. "After all these years?"

He didn't care to answer her question. "You're cold. Is she gone? Why don't we go back in."

"I should. I've probably got a line of kids at my office by now."

He opened the door and gestured her inside. Dana walked ahead of him. She hesitated a few steps in, as if she wasn't sure he'd follow.

The halls were full of fifth-graders changing classes and fourth-graders heading out to recess. She and Patrick didn't try to talk over the din. He shook his head at the clothing some of the girls wore. Nothing would have let him allow Melanie or Lissa to dress that skimpy.

And Annabelle?

He had to be honest. He would have let her wear anything if he could have had her back.

Jenny was gone from the clinic, but Dana had been right. A line of fidgety kids waited outside the office.

He watched her as she dispatched medications and did the asthma tests in record time. Once the last student was out the door, she turned to Patrick.

"What do you want?"

"Now?"

"No. What did you want earlier, when you came in." *And found Jenny* didn't have to be spoken.

"Oh, that." Patrick cracked his knuckles to buy time, and caught Dana's wince. "What? The business about knuckle cracking causing arthritis is an old wives' tale. You're a nurse. You should know that."

"Doesn't make me appreciate the sound any better." She propped herself against the counter. "So, what'd you want?"

To see you. More than I'd like to admit. He scrambled for something less revealing. "Uh, I just wanted to clarify something you said about the mold."

"Oh." She looked disappointed.

"How's the dog?"

Dana lifted her head. "Good. You saw him with Kate. He's settled right in. I'm taking him by the vet's this afternoon."

Patrick grinned at the memory of Kate with Rascal. "I hope you got some sleep."

"Not much. But the dog didn't keep me awake. You did."

The confession startled him. "What do you mean?"

Her face pinkened, and she stared at her feet. "You know what I mean. You make me want to do crazy things, like go to a pool when I know you'll be there, and let you kiss me, and kiss you back."

His palms grew damp at her honesty. "Doesn't sound so crazy to me."

"I need things to be simple right now, Patrick. And you're not simple."

"Yes, I am." He wiped his palms on his jeans, hoping like hell she didn't notice. Then he crossed over to her and cupped her face in his hands. "I can be very simple. As simple as you like. Simple's better for me."

He bent to kiss her, but she moved away with a breathy laugh. "Uh, not here. A student could waltz in. Or the principal. Or, worse, Suze."

Patrick contented himself with a very unsatisfactory kiss on the forehead. "Rain check?"

She chuckled again. "You don't give up, do you?"

"Not usually." He stepped away from her. "There. You can trust me, even if you don't trust yourself. All us guys aren't like Mr. 'You can sue—I can help.'" With that, he left her—and for once, with a smile on her face.

HE GOT HOME that night in a better frame of mind than he had been in weeks. Whether it was due to getting ahead on some work at the shop or speaking with Dana, he couldn't say. But at least some of his dark mood had lifted.

The doorbell rang as he fired up the stove under some kielbasa sausages for a quick supper. Before Patrick could turn from the cast iron frying pan, he heard Melanie call out, "Dad?"

"In the kitchen, Mel."

Her high heels clacked against the hardwood floor in the living room, sounding louder as she approached. He glanced up from the sausages to find her still in work wear—a blazer and slacks.

"Hey. Want me to put another sausage on for you?" he offered.

Mel wrinkled her nose. "Do you realize how bad those things are? Full of cholesterol and nitrites."

"Hmm, I thought they were a better choice than hot dogs," he teased.

"Anything's better than a hot dog."

"Don't fuss. I don't have them often."

She sighed. "I keep thinking I should give up on

fussing—it never does any good—but I can't seem to stop myself."

Patrick checked on the sausage. "I hear you, Mel. Honest. One thing you *can* give up on is the tofu harangue."

"Aw, and I just bought a huge value pack of the stuff. I thought you might want to share." Mel grinned. In a more serious tone, she added, "I nag because I care. I want you around for a long, long time, Dad."

"I know." He didn't promise her anything. After Annabelle, he'd learned you couldn't promise anything you didn't have control over. All you could promise anyone was this moment.

"So you'll make a point to eat your five fruits and veggies a day?" she persisted.

"Nag."

"Mule."

The old joke comforted him, put him in an even better mood. He reached for a plate and began lifting the sausage. "So how was your day? Could you hand me the mustard?"

She growled in mock irritation. "When I say add color to your diet, Dad, I don't mean ketchup and mustard."

But she followed him into the dining room, where she agreed to join him in at least a glass of tea. Which she barely touched. Patrick could tell something was on her mind, despite her earlier lightheartedness.

"What's wrong? Something at work? Not that son-in-law of mine, or I'll take my shotgun to him." Now it was Patrick who winked.

"Mom called me today."

Jenny. Patrick laid his sausage on the plate and hid

his irritation by clasping his hands in his best imperso-
nation of an unflappable Father Knows Best. "That so?"

"She said she saw you today."

"Uh, yeah. Briefly."

"And that you wigged out."

He shook his head. "I did not wig out. Seeing her
there surprised me is all. I didn't expect her."

Melanie busied her fingers making accordion folds
in the paper napkin he'd given her. "She said you were
with that nurse."

"Not exactly. Your mother was with Dana. Not me.
I just stuck my head in."

"Oh. Good." Then apprehension punctuated her momentary relief. "What were you doing there?"

Patrick found himself lying a second time about the
same visit. "Board of education stuff," he told her in his
most innocent voice.

"Oh. Good," Mel repeated. The accordion folds
completed, she began folding the napkin into a tiny
rectangle. "What's the deal with you and her?"

"Dana?"

"Yes, Dana." Mel's tone displayed a slight peevish-
ness.

"I don't know, Mel."

"Lissa said you two have gone out a couple of
times."

"No, we haven't. We wound up swimming at the
pool at the same time, thanks to your sister, but I
wouldn't call those dates."

Mel paused in her napkin folding. "Will you? Date
her, I mean."

Her eyes pinned him down. "Maybe. Is that a
problem?"

"She's got a baby, Dad."

"A toddler. We're not talking about a newborn here."

"Yes, a toddler." Mel was back to folding. The napkin was now a hard little lump. She began unfolding it.

"I've dated lots of women since your mom and I divorced. You never seemed that concerned before."

"Never a woman with a baby—toddler," she corrected hastily. "I don't want you to make a mistake, that's all. To tie yourself down."

He hid his amusement behind another sip of his tea. "Isn't this the speech I gave you a few short years ago, when your Mr. Right came knocking?"

"He was my Mr. Right. He still is. But he didn't have a baby."

"A—"

"Toddler," she amended. "Still, pretty much a helpless individual, who will be dependent on you for the foreseeable future and will set you back a heap of money for college. Or have you forgotten how expensive Lissa's tuition is?" Her grin softened her words a bit, but her eyes were unsmiling.

"No. I just wrote out another check. And I haven't forgotten how expensive your education was, either. But you two are worth it, the way I see it. Small investment. Maybe you'll bring your old man a crust of bread when he's down and out after eating one too many of these bad old kielbasas." Patrick took a bite of the sausage and focused on chewing so he wouldn't have to think about what Mel had said.

"So you agree?"

"You learn the Socratic method in college? Did I pay for that canny technique for questioning?"

"Dad! I'm making an effort to have a serious conversation here," she protested.

"And I'm making an effort to avoid it. Not working for either of us, is it?" When he saw that his joke had fallen flat, he sighed. "Mel, even if I do go on a few dates with Dana, what's the big deal? If I haven't gotten in over my head in fourteen years, then why do you think it's suddenly going to happen now?"

"I don't. I don't think, anyway. I just worry. You know that."

"My champion worrier. If the Olympics had an event in apprehension, you would win the gold." He took another bite of the sausage, which went down like a stone. He'd have heartburn after a day like this, but he didn't dare reach for the antacids until after Mel left.

"Maybe it is a big deal, Dad. Maybe you shouldn't even try dating her. I mean, is it fair to date a woman with a small child and not consider a long-term commitment?"

"Hey, she's the one who wants things simple."

Mel's fingers had moved on to shredding. The napkin was officially toast. "So you two—"

"Quit the 'so's.'" He sounded more irritated than he would have liked. "We talk. We even flirt. But the relationship's not serious. She's divorced, and she doesn't seem too interested in seeing anybody, much less waltzing down the aisle."

"Lissa appears to consider you two a perfect match."

"Well, tell her to quit drawing up an invitation list for our wedding. It's postponed indefinitely. That make you feel better?"

Mel's laugh was a reluctant one. "Why do you always try to make me laugh?"

"Because you're a worrywart, remember? You always were a sober little thing. Now, with Lissa, I try to make her worry. Doesn't do any good."

"Lissa." Mel looked skyward. "She's up to something. I don't know what she figures she'll get out of pushing the two of you together, but it's her latest project. So—and yes, I did say *so*—watch out. You know Lissa."

"She's of my gene pool, isn't she? Like you. Yes, I do know her. Now, unless you want that other piece of kielbasa or I can interest you in something else that has marginally more nutritional value, I'd suggest you beat it, kid. You've had a long day at work and an even longer day worrying about me. Go home. Kick those heels off, make that son-in-law of mine fix you supper, for a change. And that's an order."

She smiled. "Okay." After sweeping the bits and pieces of napkin into her palm, she walked to the kitchen to discard them.

When she returned, Patrick was waiting for her, "Let me escort you to the door," he said.

He made a few more jokes as he walked her out and gave her a hug. He had been glad to see her, but he had to confess that he was relieved once the taillights of her car disappeared down the driveway.

The inquisition was over. Mel made perfect sense. Classic Mel. She always made sense. She was always right.

And when it came to Dana, Mel was right yet again.

CHAPTER EIGHTEEN

DANA TURNED onto Main Street on her way to Kate's day care, NPR on the radio. She realized she was tuning out a story on *All Things Considered* when she found herself struggling to recall the story's location.

Her focus was really—well, that was simple enough. On Patrick.

But where was Patrick? That was the million-dollar-question.

In the past week and a half, he hadn't been at the pool his usual nights. She'd been there both evenings. Dana had hated how she'd stayed past her allotted time just to make sure he hadn't shown. She had managed to salvage enough of her pride not to quiz Lissa about her father's whereabouts.

Both last Friday and today, he'd e-mailed and claimed the pressures of work. He'd asked her to e-mail him the asthma reports as an attachment to her reply.

Dana had resisted the urge to be anything but strictly business. She'd sent the reports back with a cheery, "Here they are!" and a harder than necessary hit on the send key.

Despite the near kiss he'd given Dana at the clinic, he'd called her only once. That would have been the short, generic, "Sorry I'm MIA lately. Been busy" message he'd included with his e-mail request.

Dana didn't have to be clued in to what was happening. She remembered Lissa talking about those messages bewildered women had left Patrick which he'd deleted. He was one of those guys who were all about the thrill of the chase. Once his prey was in his grasp, the hunt was over and he itched to move on. Either that or he couldn't get past Kate.

Frankly, Dana didn't know which hurt most.

If only she could look at Rascal without conjuring Patrick. Perhaps she could move on, as well.

She increased the volume on the radio to blast away thoughts of him. In her current frame of mind, the programming on NPR was a much better alternative to the done-me-wrong songs on the country-music station.

As Dana took a left on Jefferson Avenue, the ringing of her cell phone barely punctuated NPR's next story about two pandas grieving for one another. She switched off the radio and fished her phone out of her bag.

"Dana?" Patrick sounded tense.

"Yes?" She went on full alert.

"Could you… I need some help. I—tripped over my own two feet and grabbed hold of a cactus, and I'm sporting a handful of thorns in my right hand. I can't manage to get the little buggers out."

"A cactus?" He hadn't called her in nearly two weeks, and when he did, it was about a cactus?

"Don't ask. It seemed like a good idea at the time."

"Okay." She didn't want to, but she chuckled. "I gather you require a house call?"

"I certainly don't feel like driving."

"Um, any *other* body parts land on that cactus?"

An embarrassed silence followed. "Thank God, no. Just my hand."

"Why do I get the feeling you wouldn't tell me,

anyway? Never mind. I'm en route to pick up Kate. Let me collect her, get my kit from home and Kate and I will be over in a few minutes."

PATRICK WAITED for them on his front porch. Dana looked up from pulling out her first-aid kit to see Kate dash for the porch and Patrick. "Wait! Kate!" Dana called out.

But Kate didn't hesitate. Her tiny legs pumped furiously as she raced up the front walk before slowing for the steps.

"Mr. Patrick? Do you got a boo-boo?" she asked.

"More than one. Are you here to help your mom?"

Dana's grip on the first-aid kit eased at his equable tone. She noticed Kate nod soberly. The kit in hand, Dana joined the pair. She knelt to meet Kate at eye-level. "Kiddo, don't run from Mommy like that, okay? It scares me. You have to stay by Mommy's side."

Kate's chin quivered. "I was just running to talk to Mr. Patrick."

"I realize that, sweetheart. But until you get older and bigger, you wait on Mommy. Got it?"

Now Kate's head dropped. "Got it."

Patrick broke the ensuing silence. "Thank you for coming. My hand is hurting like a…well, you know what. You've saved me from a somewhat embarrassing trip to the E.R. I figured if you could rescue and patch up a puppy, a few cactus thorns would—"

"Not a problem." Dana was determined to be as professional as possible. After all, if remaining incommunicado was his way of following up on a near-kiss, then obviously, she wasn't the only one in this relationship with a problem. "Let's get inside, where it's warm, and I'll de-thorn you."

At the kitchen table, under the bright fluorescent

lights, Dana opened her bag and got out her best tweezers and a magnifying glass. "Let's have a peek at that hand."

With evident hesitation, he presented the wounded appendage. It was covered in dozens of cacti thorns. "This won't hurt, will it?"

"Wow! You weren't kidding." She bent to her work and started plucking out the thorns. "This is worse than Rascal's cut."

Kate crowded in. "Let me, Mommy! I wanna! Please? I'm *good* at helping!"

"Not just yet, baby. Let Mommy see, okay? Move back."

"But—but—" Kate whimpered, then tried to catch her bottom lip before it started trembling.

Patrick completely shocked Dana by swinging Kate up on his lap with his good hand. "Maybe you can help your mom pick the next one she's going to pluck out."

"Can I, Mommy? Can I?"

Dana shot him a glance. "Are you sure, Patrick?"

Her question had apparently touched too close to a tender spot. He raised one eyebrow, his eyes glittering with challenge. "Of course I am. Why on earth would I have a problem holding Kate?"

Oh, just because you get all shaken up whenever you're around her.

But Dana didn't argue with him. It was his choice. "Okay, baby girl. As long as you stay still, out of my line of sight. And don't get on these thorns. Then I'd have to pluck them out of you."

As Dana worked, steadily reducing the number of thorns, she couldn't keep herself from noticing Patrick's hand. The fingers were long, with calluses from the manual labor he did, but they still appeared sensitive. She let her own fingers glide over skin not punctured with thorns and felt him respond by pressing back.

"You're making good progress," he told her.

"Thanks." Guilty at being caught caressing him, Dana returned her focus to supplying first aid. "So you grabbed a cactus."

"Yeah, in the backyard. The girls planted this cactus somebody sent us in some flower-of-the-month deal. I tripped over the garden hose and grabbed for anything to break my fall."

"Looks like the cactus grabbed back. At least I won't have to dig these thorns out of your, uh, tush."

Patrick's face pinkened. "I gather you've had to do that in your official capacity."

"Shoot, yeah. It wasn't the Christmas holidays if a couple of drunk good ol' boys didn't come in after shoving each other into the Christmas cactus they had lying around. But everybody's backside looks the same—" She broke off and struggled not to think about how Patrick's backside was like no good ol' boy's she'd ever yanked cacti thorns out of. Now *her* face pinkened.

She resumed her task, grasping a thorn, pulling, tapping the tweezers against the napkin she had spread out. From the corner of her eye, she saw Kate getting restless, then Patrick's good hand reaching up to ruffle her daughter's hair.

Dana could only stare. Patrick's fingers froze in mid-pat. Slowly, he dropped his hand and put it on the table. With that, Dana yanked her attention back to the thorns.

He cleared his throat. "Thanks for e-mailing me the reports," Patrick said.

She was glad of the change in subject, even if the

new topic was much more unpleasant. "Of course. You've been busy, huh?"

"The shop's overflowing with cars, and I had two contractors order windows this week. Plus all the work the school board generates. I guess I shouldn't complain."

Too busy to pick up the phone and call me? She started tweezing the few remaining thorns.

Patrick winced at her aggressive tug to get the last thorn out. "Ow!"

"All done."

He inspected his palm. "*You* didn't phone *me*. I thought you were probably as busy as I was."

Dana flushed at the memory of her indecision over whether to call him. She would die of mortification if he knew how many times she'd picked up the phone to do so.

"I figured that if you needed me for anything, you knew where to find me," was her only response. She busied herself putting away her tools.

"Something I said?" Patrick prompted when she didn't volunteer anything further.

Something you didn't. Dana wanted this Patrick, the one who could be a tease around her with Kate. But he hadn't called her. The silence had echoed strongly with Marty's love 'em and leave 'em approach. Maybe that wasn't fair. Maybe Patrick was nowhere near the sort of man Marty was.

Then again, maybe he was.

PATRICK SET DOWN KATE. "There you go, punchinello." He bit his lip at the slip. She wasn't Annabelle. He'd convinced himself of that in the few short minutes of having her in his lap.

No, Annabelle would have run screaming from any

instrument that bore a resemblance to medical equipment. His little one had been squeamish about all things to do with a doctor long before she'd gotten sick.

The stark difference between Kate's fascination with her mother's thorn-removal and what would have been Annabelle's reaction had helped him over those first agonizing few moments.

"You're a good assistant, Kate," he told her.

She nodded soberly again. "I'm gonna be a doctor when I grow up. My mommy says doctors are the boss."

He chucked her chin with his good hand. "Your mommy says that, huh? Sounds like she knows a thing or two about doctors."

Dana's face pinkened anew. "Guess I was a little too honest around her."

"Kids are better than a truth serum, that's for sure. I wonder."

"What?"

"If I asked her what you've said about me, what would she tell me?"

Now Dana's cheeks went from pink to scarlet. "*That* I don't talk about in front of her."

He pushed his chair back and headed for the kitchen sink. As the cold water rushed over his hands and stung the dozens of places where the thorns had been, he thought better of his words to Dana.

Glancing over his shoulder, he took in the bemused expression on her face. The past few days, he'd had such good follow-through on letting his attraction for her fade. Yet the flimsiest excuse, he'd called her to rescue him. He could have called Mel. He should have.

The doorbell rang before he could make up his mind how to handle the situation he found himself in. He knew exactly who was at the door.

"Aw, shoot. Is it five already? That will be Vann."

How the heck he'd explain this one to his buddy, he wasn't certain. But he was already betting his explanation would wind up a story in Vann's repertoire, never to be forgotten.

CHAPTER NINETEEN

PATRICK MADE a beeline for the front door and opened it. Vann stood there, a grocery bag in his hands, a big cardboard box at his feet and puzzlement in his eyes.

"Did I get the night wrong? I see you have company." He nodded toward Dana's Pacifica.

"No, no. It's cold out." Patrick stepped back and ushered Vann in. "While I was trying to light the grill, I tripped on the garden hose and landed in that cactus plant Mel and Lissa planted. I have to confess—I don't have the steaks on the grill yet."

A pained look stole over on Vann's face. Patrick couldn't decide whether it stemmed from empathy for his fall or a frustrated appetite.

"What's in the box?" Patrick nudged the cardboard with the toe of his shoe.

"I don't know. The UPS guy just dropped it off. Said he didn't need a signature. So whose car?"

Patrick waited for Vann to edge by him in the door, then knelt to examine the box. "Shoot. Mel sent me a Christmas tree. I told her not to waste her money—it's not like she and Luke have pots of it."

"The car?" Vann prompted again from just inside the door.

"Oh, that's Dana's. I had to call her to help out with the thorns."

Vann's eyes twinkled with amusement. "Had to, huh? What exact part of your anatomy landed in that bush, anyway? And are you still able to cook?"

"My hand, you pervert! Get inside. The steaks won't take that long."

"Hey, buddy, you were the one who wanted to grill steaks in the dead of winter. I can do with a pizza or three."

Patrick lugged the tree box into the kitchen, with Vann preceding him. Dana was gathering up her kit. She had that leaving expression written all over her.

Things would certainly be easier if she and Kate did leave. Less ammunition for Vann, who took in the scene with open curiosity. But Patrick found himself not wanting to do the easy thing.

"No, don't go, Dana. You and Kate should join us. I've got plenty. It'll be fast once the charcoal gets going."

Vann blinked at Patrick's words to Dana.

You're surprised, buddy? I flabbergast myself sometimes.

Vann recovered more quickly than Dana, who still appeared dubious. He dropped the grocery bag on the table with some good-natured ribbing. "If, that is, our friend the klutz can manage to *start* the charcoal. Man, the times I saved his butt when he was a skinny quarterback and I had to block for him."

Patrick rolled his eyes. "What do you say, Dana?"

"I always seem to be barging in on you at special occasions." Dana hadn't put the kit back down on the table, but she hadn't stowed it in her bag, either.

"This? A special occasion?" Vann's laughter boomed. "This is two bachelors having a steak on a Friday night. Or it would have been. Don't worry on my part."

Silence billowed around them. To cover his awkwardness, Patrick rubbed his palms together briskly, then grimaced at the pain.

Kate toddled over to the carton, which was nearly as big as she was. "I open?" she asked.

"No, honey," Dana told her. She'd begun gathering up her things, and Kate's coat dangled from her fingertips. "Put on your coat. That's not yours. That's Mr. Patrick's."

Vann chuckled again. "That box is Mel's way of telling Patrick he'll have Christmas, and by golly, he'll enjoy it."

"Huh?" Dana had Kate corralled and was wrestling her into the coat.

"I enjoy Christmas," Patrick protested. "I just don't go overboard."

"Right." Vann nodded. "This box—like all the ones before it—testifies to your dedication regarding the holiday spirit."

"What is in that box?" Dana's brow wrinkled. "What—you order Christmas presents online?"

Before Patrick could say anything, Vann's laugh, now big and round and filling the kitchen, interrupted him yet again. "Patrick? Patrick is the king of the gift card. Or the fifty-dollar bill. No. *That*—" Vann pointed to the box "—is Patrick's Christmas tree."

"A Kissmus tree!" Kate shouted joyously. "I want to open it! Mommy! It's a Kissmus tree!"

Patrick sighed and rubbed his face with the palm of his good hand. He sagged against the kitchen counter. "Mel feels it's important I actually have a tree. So every year, she orders me one of those Norfolk pines from some exorbitantly expensive catalog. And every year I kill the pine."

"He's wanted for tree-icide in all fifty states," Vann agreed.

"You're not helping. I thought you were supposed to be my friend," Patrick complained.

"And friends can't tell it like it is?"

Kate had shed her coat and was attempting to rip into the box. Dana pulled her back. "No. It's not yours."

"Let her. I don't mind." Patrick fumbled in a drawer for a pair of scissors. He crouched beside Kate and began cutting the carton.

"Ooh, snow!" Kate shrieked as foam noodles exploded out of the box. She began tossing them in the air, and they rained down on her and Dana and Patrick.

Patrick sliced through the cardboard. The sides of the box fell away to reveal a drooping little pine covered in brave scarlet bows.

They all stared the unprepossessing tree, not saying anything. Then Kate spoke. "Mr. Patrick, the snow was neat. But your Kissmus tree doesn't look happy."

She was right, Patrick realized. And the tree didn't just look unhappy—it looked downright pathetic. Had last year's version been this sad?

Kate fingered one of the bows. "Your tree doesn't have any lights." She skewered Patrick with a pitying expression. "Santa won't even know it's a Kissmus tree."

"Kate." Dana put a hand on her daughter's shoulder, then bent to whisper in Kate's ear, but Patrick heard anyway. "We shouldn't hurt people's feelings. That's Mr. Patrick's tree, and he may like it."

"But Mommy! Santa *won't* know." Kate's brow furrowed.

"Santa knows everything."

"Hey. It's okay. She's right." Patrick tried without

success to straighten the leaning potted tree. "It's not much of a tree. Mel will be disappointed."

"It's the thought that counts," Dana said diplomatically.

"We're gonna have a *better* tree." As Kate confided this to Patrick, she wrapped her fingers around his arm. "It's gonna be the biggest ever, and Mommy said I can put the angel on top. Mommy will have to help, but I get to do it. When we go, maybe we can get you a better tree."

Patrick's throat closed up on him. Was it from Kate's touch or from memories of Christmases past? Or was it just from looking at that pitiful tree?

"What do you say we skip the steaks?" Patrick blurted out.

Vann reacted with predictable alarm. "No supper?"

"We can grab something on the way." He let his fingers slip through the limp branches.

"And where are we going?" Vann asked.

"I know!" Kate jumped up and down, making the tree shimmy on the floor. "We're gonna get a tree! We're gonna get a Kissmus tree!"

Vann stuffed the unpacked bag of groceries into the fridge. "Forget the steaks. This I've got to see."

DANA STOOD shivering in the cold, windy alley between the rows of Christmas trees. Kate didn't seem to mind the cold, but then she was leading Patrick by the hand at a near run from tree to tree.

"This one! Get this one!" Kate was telling him, only to say a few minutes later, "No, Mr. Patrick, this one is bigger!"

Vann stood by her, equally impervious to the chill in the air. "I would have never believed it."

"Just how long has it been since Patrick bought a Christmas tree?"

"Uh, good question." Vann chewed on his lower lip in concentration. "Probably the year Annabelle died. Jenny and he split up, and the girls stayed with her. He had a little apartment, not big enough to swing a cat in. He claimed then that he didn't have the room, but he didn't get a tree even when he bought the house he's in now."

Dana recalled the spick-and-span kitchen, with its fridge door devoid of children's drawings, and its pristine white cabinets. Patrick's place hadn't experienced the sticky fingerprints of a child. Somehow that made her sadder than the tree had.

"No Christmas tree in how many years—fourteen?" Dana shook her head. She breathed in the heady smell of the evergreens and wondered how a person could even feel Christmas without such scents filling the house.

"Not unless you count Mel's contributions." Van ambled down the path between the rows of trees. "Aren't you supposed to be picking out one?"

"Already got it covered. I told the owner I wanted that beauty over there, and I'm going to tell Kate that Santa chose it especially for her."

"So how will you convince Kate it's Santa's pick?" Vann asked.

She pulled a big fat candy cane out of her purse. "Bought it from the owner when I paid for the tree," she said. "I put the candy cane on, and it's a sure sign from Santa."

Vann grinned at her. "A canny lass, you are, and wickedly manipulative."

"No, no. I learned my lesson about running around

a tree farm last year. That's all." She heard Kate pronounce yet another tree perfect, heard her chuckles as her daughter led Patrick to inspect it. Dana fished out some twine from her purse and began working a loop around the end of the candy cane. "Was it rough?"

Vann stopped, turned. "You mean losing Annabelle? It was the worst thing I've ever gone through. Patrick was a zombie. Until the funeral."

"What happened?" Dana concentrated on tying one end of the string to a twig of her tree. Her fingers trembled each time she attempted to fasten the knot.

"He wouldn't let them close the coffin. Nobody, and I mean nobody, was going to shut that coffin. He freaked. I thought he was having a nervous breakdown. That we would have to cart him out of that funeral home in a straitjacket."

Dana shivered and the twig snapped off in her fingers. She sighed and reached for another twig, beginning the whole process anew. "But he got through it."

"Yeah. I suppose. Does anybody have any choice but to get through it? It's not like you can change something like that."

She glanced over to check on Kate. She was still chugging through the trees, Patrick in tow. With care, Dana framed the question rolling around in her mind. "If he hasn't adjusted in all these years, do you think he ever will?"

Again she concentrated on tying the string. Vann moved to stand beside her and held out a hand for the twine. "Here. Let me. You obviously weren't an Eagle Scout."

"And you were?"

"Me and Patrick. The dynamic duo."

Dana handed him the candy cane, with its twine leash, and watched him secure it to the tree. "You asked about Patrick and if he'd ever…" Vann straightened the bright red-and-white cane to show it off to its best advantage. "Maybe. I can't say for sure. Nobody can. A child's death is not something a person ever gets over, I'd guess. But he's here. Buying a Christmas tree. That's more progress than I've seen in years."

Now Dana spied Kate on Patrick's shoulders, high above the treetops, giggling. Amazing. Maybe there was a chance.

"Why has it taken years, when Jenny was obviously able to move on?"

"I don't know. Patrick never talks about it. Not even with me. Sometimes I can tell it's getting to him. But this part of his life everybody here understands not to mess with. And if you do, you get the rough side of Mel's tongue. She's very protective of him, you know."

Dana recalled those dagger eyes, and the way Patrick had attempted to soothe her on the phone. Oh, Dana knew all about how protective Mel was.

"Mommy! We found it! We found Mr. Patrick's tree!" Patrick and Kate burst through the wall of trees down from where Vann and Dana stood. Kate still rode atop Patrick's shoulders.

"You did?" Dana scrutinized Patrick for signs of distress. All she could detect was bemusement, as though he'd been poleaxed. His breath arrived in gasps, the air cool enough that wisps formed with each exhalation. "How'd you know?"

"A bird's nest! And I get to keep the nest!"

Patrick eased Kate down. "Enough," he said in a quiet voice. It held no trace of scolding, just a firm limit, as though he'd had all he wanted of a helping of pie and would have no more.

Enough. Dana swallowed, her earlier optimism fading. But she didn't have a chance to analyze her emotions. Kate was tugging at her hand to show her the tree.

She cast a smile over her shoulder as she allowed herself to be led away. Kate found the tree and began pointing out the multitude of reasons it was just right. Dana gazed at her daughter's blond curls and her animated features through an unexpected mist of tears.

Kate was beautiful. Funny. Smart. Generous. Sure, Dana was her mom, but even she could honestly say Kate was all that. So why was one little human being—so precious to Dana—enough to scare men away? And would Dana ever find a man who didn't mind a two-for-one deal?

PATRICK'S HAND SHOOK as he pulled out the cash to pay the tree-farm owner.

"What am I doing?" he asked Vann.

"Starving me to death. If we don't hurry and get this tree—these trees—loaded up, I just might perish."

"Sorry, man. I don't know what got into me. Buying a dumb tree. I don't even have any decorations for it." Patrick drummed his fingers on the rough wooden counter of the tree-farm office as he waited for the owner to finish shaking the tree and wrapping it in netting.

"Bet Mel could help you with that."

"Oh, God," Patrick groaned. "I don't even want to *face* Mel. How am I going to explain another Christmas tree?"

Vann propped his foot on the rung of a stool. "It's not like you did something wrong, Patrick."

"Yeah, well, this will require a lot of fast talking. Especially after she gave me one of her 'don't get involved with a woman with kids' speeches."

The whir and grind of the tree-shaker started up. Patrick gazed out the window, and saw Dana with Kate on her hip, pointing out the intricacies of the machine to the little girl.

Vann's reply was lost in the noise. Just as well. Patrick couldn't focus on anything but Dana and Kate.

The machine quieted. "You okay?" Vann had dispensed with his usual wisecracking.

"Sure." What else could Patrick say? That toting Kate around on his shoulders was the most exquisite torture he'd ever endured?

Why the hell did Dana have to come along and show me what I didn't have?

CHAPTER TWENTY

DANA EYED THE TREE in its stand and nodded. "Yep, that will do. It's not leaning much."

Patrick backed up to view the tree from beside her. "No. It's crooked."

Vann scoffed from where he knelt by the tree. He placed a hand on the small of his back and groaned dramatically. "Now I know why you haven't bothered with a tree all these years—your perfectionistic streak. The lady says it's fine, so it's fine."

"It's crooked." Patrick frowned. "We need to move it to the right about, uh, two inches."

"Next you'll be running a plumb line. Look, buddy, you promised me steak, and now…"

But Dana could tell there was no bite to Vann's grumbling. He and Patrick wiggled the tree in its stand in her living room.

"Can we decorate it, Mommy? Tonight? I'll help."

"No, sweetheart. Tomorrow, okay? It's time for your bath." Dana braced herself for an onslaught of protest, but all Kate did was sigh.

They had stopped at the Chinese takeout place on the way to Dana's. Her treat, she'd told Patrick and Vann. It was the least she could do for their assistance with the tree. Vann had assured her she was a saint, because she'd overridden Patrick's protests that they could do without food.

She left the two men to their meaningless bickering about the tree, with Rascal barking and growling at this new and strange addition to the living room. After giving Kate the world's quickest bath, she started laying out supper.

The impromptu meal turned out far differently than Dana had feared it would. Patrick seemed more approachable and less tense than he had at the tree farm. And Vann—well, Vann obviously had great affection for Patrick, despite all the joking he did.

What friend did Dana have who would have stuck around the way Vann had for Patrick? She'd waited so long to have kids that all her old girlfriends from college had moved on to other acquaintances with more in common. Then, when Dana had become pregnant with Kate, Dana's childless friends had one by one fallen to the wayside.

Her feeling of isolation and loneliness had been one reason she'd made the move to Logan. Dana had craved the small-town intimacy people always talked about.

She liked the people of Logan. They'd welcomed her and Kate into their fold, shared advice, the odd cup of sugar, elbow grease.

Dana nearly dropped her chopsticks when the ring tone of the *Monday Night Football* theme cut through the air. Whipping her head around to where it came from, she heard Vann sigh.

"Knew an uninterrupted Friday night was too good to be true." He fished out his cell phone and pressed it against his ear.

Dana took stock of Kate, noticed she was playing with her fried rice rather than eating it. Superhighways dissected the hills and valleys of rice on the plate. After pushing back her chair, Dana grabbed her own plate and let Kate have a few more minutes pretending to be a transportation engineer.

On her way to the sink she heard Vann say, "When?" Then, "How bad? Anybody hurt?"

Dana met Patrick's eyes. The worry in them made her drop the plate into the sink. He crossed the kitchen to stand beside her.

"What should I do with the leftovers?" he asked.

He said something else, but she didn't hear it. Instead, she was lost in the smell of him, in the spruce and cold wind from the outdoors still clinging to him. He'd come too close to her again.

Touch me. No. Don't.

"Sorry, folks. Party's over."

Vann's pronouncement made her jump back guiltily.

"What's wrong?" Patrick asked.

"Steam pipe in the elementary school lunchroom burst. Not sure what happened. The fire department got called in when someone thought they saw smoke."

"But it wasn't a fire?" Dana switched on the water, rinsed the plate.

"Nope. Whole place was full of steam." Vann pressed his palms down on the table and stood. "I'll head over there."

Steam. If there hadn't been mold in the lunchroom before, there would be now—or at least, a good start on it.

"Hold on, and I'll ride with you." Patrick had begun clearing the table, quickly ferrying the left-overs to the fridge. The only thing remaining was Kate's plate.

Dana saw his hesitancy about approaching Kate and realized that he'd filled his time at the table talking with Vann, not Kate.

Dana took three swift steps to Kate's side. "Sweetheart? Done?"

"Can I have a treat?"

"Absolutely—if you eat two more bites of your rice."

That engendered a whole lot of moaning and groaning, but Kate did as she was told. Dana was wiping down the counters when Patrick asked, "Want to come along, Dana?"

Did she? The smart thing would be to stay home. It was late, Kate was tired and there was nothing for Dana to do at the school.

Dana hesitated, then relented. "Okay," she said. She acknowledged then that where Patrick was concerned, she'd never find it easy to say no to him. Just another reason to stay a long, long way from him.

DESPITE THE MAMMOTH ventilation fans set up at the exits, the steam still clung in the air when they arrived at the school. The lunchroom was as muggy as on a hot July day.

"Watch your step. That floor's slick," cautioned Logan's fire chief Eddie Brumley. "Two of my guys have gone down on it already."

"What caused the burst?" Patrick asked.

"Radiator on this inside wall sprang a leak, from what we can tell. Boiler apparently malfunctioned, and the pressure built up."

"Thank God no kids were here when it happened." Vann swiped at a face already damp with perspiration despite the cool temperature he'd just walked in from.

"You've got that right. Scalding hot water and steam burns would be nasty."

"Damage?"

Eddie shrugged. "Not much on the scale of things.

Mostly it's a matter of mopping up the water on the floor and wiping down all this condensation on the walls. And getting the boiler fixed, of course."

Vann sighed. "Thing's nearly obsolete. I've got one company I can call on to fix it. The last time they came, they charged me the earth. Guess I'd better phone and see if I can get them here."

He turned away, leaving Patrick and Dana, with Kate on her hip, surveying the flooded lunchroom.

"That's got to be an inch and a half of water still in there." Dana shifted Kate in her arms.

Dana looked uncomfortable and tired. Not thinking, Patrick reached over for Kate. "Here. Let me hold her."

Too late, he realized his mistake. Still, he allowed Kate's head to loll against his shoulder. To cover up his awkwardness, he asked Eddie, "How much water did you find when you got here?"

"At least two inches. It was halfway up the base-board. But when we cut off the boiler and opened the doors, the water level started going down. I don't think you'll need a pump or anything. Probably just a couple of those wet-dry vacs."

Patrick smoothed Kate's silky curls under his hand and tried to think logistics—what to do with a whole school full of children if they couldn't get this lunch-room open by Monday. Sack lunches in the classroom?

He'd forgotten how soft a child's curls could be.

Patrick yanked his thoughts back from where they were heading. "We need a new school. This one is falling down around our ears." He kicked at the water, splashing it up on the leg of his jeans. It was still plenty warm, and the dollars-and-cents part of him cursed the electricity wasted on superheating that water.

"Patrick."

Dana's use of his name, full of hesitation and apprehension, caught his attention.

"Yeah?"

"This amount of steam and water is a perfect recipe for mold. The school system should either find some mobile units or get a mold abatement company to—"

"We don't have the money." He regretted interrupting her. "Listen, we'll get the water vacuumed up as soon as possible, open the doors, let the lunchroom dry out."

"That steam penetrated every corner of this room. You've got the dropped ceiling, the tile floor, the stage curtains, the nooks and crannies."

"She has a point." Eddie's echo aggravated him. "If you've got any mold in here at all, that moisture kick-started it. It was nearly a hundred degrees when we opened the door, and there was so much steam, it looked like pea soup. Plus, we've got rain forecasted for the first of the week, so you won't have any dry air for a while. You reintroduce heat in here, and bingo."

"Before we can reintroduce heat, we've got to get the boiler going. Which, from the look on Vann's face, might not be anytime soon."

Another firefighter called Eddie away from them. Patrick stared at the mess and adjusted his hold on Kate to keep her head from sliding off his shoulder. The county's parents and kids were depending on him to fix this. Cleanup would mean overtime pay for custodians. Boiler repairs would mean an emergency service call charge and God only knows how much in parts and labor.

Dana spoke up again. "This would be the perfect time, Patrick. When you've got the lunchroom shut down anyway."

"What part of 'no money' don't you understand?" His sharp tone had roused Kate. He blew out a breath to calm himself. "Shh, honey. Sorry. Go back to sleep."

"Here. Give her to me." Dana's words were cool. "We should go. Obviously, you don't need my advice or input. Not when you've already made up your mind."

Kate reached for her mother's arms. With a reluctance that surprised him, he relinquished the child. "Dana, don't be like this."

"Like what, Patrick?" Dana circled protective arms around her daughter.

"We had a good evening. Didn't we?" He jammed empty hands into his pockets.

"We did." Her chin lifted; her mouth tightened. "But that doesn't have anything to do with this. You can cut all the corners you want to, but sometimes the savings up front will result in greater costs in the end. Go to the board and get the money needed to fix the problem properly. Don't take no for an answer."

"But they can still say no." Patrick sagged against the door frame, which was still wet with condensation. "We just don't have a yes. We may never get it."

"That's true." Resignation tinged her voice.

For a moment, Patrick hoped she'd seen things his way. The anger on her face had dissipated, along with the tension that had held her rigid.

She dashed his hope by turning away. Something in how her shoulders drooped as she started down the breezeway to the main building made him realize that her resignation was far scarier to him than her anger.

"Dana?"

Dana pivoted to him. "You're right. We don't have it. We never will."

She spun around and continued walking. And Patrick grasped that the "we" she was talking about was Patrick and Dana.

CHAPTER TWENTY-ONE

PATRICK'S GRIP on his pencil tightened to the point that he was afraid he'd snap it in two. He laid it beside the stack of papers on the board table. Drawing in a deep breath, he stared down the length of the table at his fellow board of education members. Curtis and Evans glowered back.

"Let me say it again, just as I did at the emergency meeting we had after the boiler accident happened." Patrick tried for deliberate calm, no emotions, despite the fact that he wanted to throw the whole mess at the two of them and tell them to fix it. "The boiler for the lunchroom is shot. It's winter. We can't go without heat in there. You've got in front of you the final bids on the repairs. To repair the boiler will set us back ten grand. And that's if we can find the parts. It is time, gentlemen. Time for us to bite the bullet and put a school bond referendum before the voters. We need a new facility."

"Because of a broken boiler?" Evans shook his head. "I said it at that first meeting you convened. Let's just fix the boiler and call it quits. To that end, why don't we just install some portable heaters? Or a new heat system?"

Patrick closed his eyes, opened them and met Vann's. Vann gave the slightest shrug, as if to say, *Go ahead, for what good it will do you.*

"Evans, repairing the boiler and calling it quits is the kind of thinking that led to the mess we're in now."

"The mess you say we're in. The school's been good enough for hundreds of kids, and it's better than what a lot of kids all over the country have. It's not the school that makes the education." Curtis leaned back and clasped his hands behind his head. "I've got voters in my district who haven't had kids in school since the seventies. They won't be happy about a property tax increase for a new school. Not when they're not getting any use out of it."

The upside-down logic assaulted Patrick. He jabbed his finger at Evans. "Whoa. That makes no sense whatsoever. I don't care if they haven't had kids in school in thirty years—education is everybody's responsibility. The kids they had in school in the seventies were educated with funds raised from voters who hadn't had kids in school since the forties, and I'll bet those voters didn't complain."

"Yeah, but they're dead and gone now, and the ones I have voting for me *are* complaining. Get real, Patrick. Give up on this. There are cheaper ways to address the lunchroom issue."

Patrick slumped in his chair. He rubbed his eyes. "Fine. You figure them out, then. Because I sure can't." With that, he called for a motion to adjourn.

Vann remained at the table after the room had emptied. "So that's it? I'm still without the funds to fix the boiler? We can't keep doing sack lunches in the classrooms, Patrick. You know that."

"Tell them. I've told them until I'm blue in the face. Face it, Vann. Until you get Curtis and Evans off this board, nothing of any good is going to happen."

"Kids can't wait on you to play nice with others, Patrick."

Patrick exploded. "Me play nice?"

"I meant all of you. The collective you. I know you're trying. But space heaters in the corners when we've got three more months of winter?"

Patrick started stacking his files and notepad. He was tired beyond exhaustion from worrying over this. It was like being tasked with creating a flock of birds when you had neither the chicken nor the egg. For two weeks now, the students had been eating sack lunches at their desks because the lunchroom was too cold without heat. He kept praying for a warm front to move through, but then he'd have to worry about Dana's prediction regarding the mold.

Dana. She'd disappeared off the face of the earth, or so it seemed. She wasn't at the pool anymore. She e-mailed him the asthma reports. When he phoned her house, Kate's little voice cut into him with her request to "Leave a message and we'll call you right back."

He always hung up before the beep. Dana couldn't be gone every time he phoned her. Obviously, she was ducking his calls.

Patrick thought about the last night they were together, the night they'd gone for the tree and the boiler had malfunctioned. She'd been so disappointed in him. That naked Christmas tree he had to water every day condemned him as much as if Dana herself had been in his living room.

Couldn't Dana understand that he was doing the best he could? Okay, so he was just a man, a school-board member who knew what the best choice was but who couldn't afford it. If the call were his, he'd level the school and build a new one. But the call wasn't his. It was the call of voters, some of whom hadn't had kids in school since the friggin' seventies.

Vann had left him alone with his thoughts, and Patrick swept his eyes across the now deserted boardroom. Sticking this out was useless. He was doing nobody any good. Maybe the voters really weren't interested in a new school. Maybe they weren't even that interested in providing the county's children with a decent education.

Patrick left the board office without talking to Vann again, afraid he'd be too tempted to tell the superintendent he was resigning. Outside, the night was cold, and from the smoke in the air, someone had been burning leaves against city ordinances.

A shape detached itself from a car in the parking lot. Patrick couldn't make it out at first. But then it approached him and he realized with a start that it was Dana.

"Hi." A simple greeting that blew him away just because it was from Dana and she was here.

"Hi," he replied. "I didn't expect to see you at school tonight. Did I miss you in the audience?"

"No. I stayed out. Rumor had it that you were going to have a knock-down-drag-out with the other board members to get the money."

Patrick dug his hands deep into his pockets and toed the cement walkway. "Rumor lied."

"Not what I heard from the folks who were there." Dana pulled her jacket around her more tightly and nodded toward the board office behind them.

"Well, let's put it this way. Telling Curtis and Evans the bottom line doesn't do any good. I still don't have money for even the boiler in the lunchroom."

"What made you do it in the first place?"

"Do what—ask again?" He shrugged. "You."

"Me?" Her mouth parted in surprise.

"When the boiler broke, you were so certain that I

should ask. That I could get the money, not just for first aid but to make things better and safer for the kids. I disappointed you. So I tried to make it up to you, and I still wound up letting you down."

"Want to talk about it?"

He shrugged. "I may resign."

Now Dana was truly shocked. "Why? Then you're just giving them what they want."

"Something Vann said tonight. Can we go sit in my truck? It's cold, plus if I stand here long enough, somebody will stop and chew me out."

"Okay."

Patrick wondered why she was being so amenable. What had she heard at school that made her give him a second chance? Or maybe she hadn't written him off in the first place.

In his truck, he switched on the ignition and let the engine warm up enough to turn the heater on. As he fiddled with the controls, Dana curved toward him in the passenger seat.

"What did Vann say?" she prompted. "To make you think you should resign?"

"He said that the kids couldn't wait on us board members to play nice. He's right. I'm thinking maybe that it's some sort of power play between me and Curtis and Evans. If it were somebody else, maybe they wouldn't feel the need to oppose the measure so strongly."

"You believe that?"

"No." He drummed his fingers on the steering wheel and stared out into the blue night.

"Then you're considering your resignation just because you're tired of fighting?" For the first time that evening, he heard disappointment in her voice.

"I am tired. I feel worse than useless. I cannot tell

you the number of times I've brought up a motion to have a school bond referendum. And I always get voted down."

"Maybe you're not trying in the right way."

"What other way is there to do it, Dana?" He didn't meet her eyes, just kept staring out the windshield at the now-darkened board office. "You ask. You explain and *then* you ask. You beg. You yell. You shout. And then finally you just give the hell up."

"Let me think on it."

"You do that. I'll go ahead and work on my letter of resignation."

Her hand brushed his cheek. "Don't quit. You'd hate yourself. You're no quitter."

Patrick turned toward her now and captured her hand in his. "You certainly have changed your opinion of me in two weeks."

"No."

"You haven't?"

"I haven't had to. I've never thought you were a quitter—not on the mold, at any rate. Just that you wanted to fix things your way. You like the full-frontal assault, and you approach things with the subtlety of a sledgehammer." She smiled. "You're not big on compromise."

"You aren't, either. I guess I can see why. In a compromise, everyone loses."

She laughed. "I concede the point. I can be pretty stubborn. You remind me of Kate, with all your 'everyone loses' talk. Are you sure you're not three?"

As soon as she'd said the words, he heard her quick intake of breath and, in that, her uncertainty about whether she should have mentioned Kate at all.

"How is she?"

Now it was Dana who wouldn't meet his eyes. "She's fine. She asks about your hand."

He squeezed her hand with his newly healed one. "Good as new. Thanks to her mom."

"Well. That's great. I guess I'd better get back. Lissa's watching Kate for me. I wanted to tell you thanks. For trying."

"Even if I didn't get you your mobile units or the money to eradicate every scrap of mold?"

"Even if." She would have slid back out into the night, but Patrick stopped her.

He put a finger under her chin, tilted her face up to his. "This is just thanks?"

"Yeah. All it needs to be, don't you think?"

"No. I don't think that at all." Patrick took a chance then and kissed her.

The kiss was supposed to be an easy one, nothing too intense. But somehow his intentions went awry the minute his mouth met hers and she kissed him back. The kiss changed not just because she felt perfect in his arms. It was that she'd come here tonight, waited for him. As though she believed he could actually accomplish something that mattered.

His hands were on her waist, underneath that way-too-cumbersome coat of hers. He couldn't seem to stop himself from inching a hand under the hem of her T-shirt. His thumb found skin silky and touchable and begging him to explore more.

Now he encircled her waist and pulled her closer to him. Her own hands were not idle. They skimmed his back, and he felt their heat through the fabric of his shirt.

He could get lost in Dana if he let himself. And tonight he wanted to, and to take hours doing it.

Before he could ask her if she wanted to get lost, too, headlights made a swath across the dim interior, freezing Dana and him in an undesired spotlight. Patrick drew back, shaded his eyes against the glare.

Then the lights bounced off into another direction and he blinked in the sudden darkness. When his eyes had adjusted, he saw Mel's car peeling out of the parking lot.

CHAPTER TWENTY-TWO

AT PATRICK'S MUTTERED expletive, Dana sat back and began hurriedly straightening her clothes. "Oh, great. I feel like I'm sixteen and I've been caught parking. Did they see us?"

"That was Mel. And yeah, it's a safe bet she did. What was she doing here? She never bothers with board meetings."

"Mel?" Dana put a hand to her forehead. "Patrick. I am so sorry. This has to be incredibly awkward for you."

He stared out the driver's-side window. "Yeah. Especially when I assured her just the other day that we weren't dating."

"Oh." Dana wasn't sure what comment to make. She sighed, remembering Jenny's warning about Mel and Lissa being at odds. "I should let you go so you can talk to her."

"About what? That she just caught her old man doing what he said he'd kill guys for if they did it with her? The other night, Mel was sounding more like the parent than me. I have no idea what to say to her, but I guess you're right. I do need to say something. Maybe apologize."

Dana touched his hand as it flexed along the steering wheel. "You're adept at that."

"Had a lot of practice lately."

"I didn't come here to—" She exhaled, searching for words. "I hoped at least to be your friend. That's what I came for."

"I'm glad you stayed for the other."

"Even if it causes trouble between you and Mel?"

She didn't like the furrow etched between his eyebrows. It shouted doubt, and she didn't want to hear doubt after the kiss he'd bestowed. She wanted to believe that she'd kissed the last frog years ago, and that Patrick was really and truly her prince.

He didn't answer her. He didn't have to. Clearly his mind was elsewhere, down the road, struggling to figure out how to defuse the situation with Mel.

"Goodbye, Patrick." Dana waited on no promises he might feel inclined to make but wouldn't be able to keep.

WHEN PATRICK COULDN'T reach Mel on her cell phone, he drove across town to her house. The windows were dark, the porch light not on.

He parked at the curb. She had to return home sometime. Where would she go at this hour of the night? And it wasn't as if she'd caught him doing something scandalous. A kiss in a truck—that wasn't so bad, was it? He was single. Dana was single.

Lights hit his rearview mirror, and Patrick straightened to check if it was Mel. He slumped again when the streetlights revealed it was just Luke in his state trooper car.

Patrick watched his son-in-law park the car in the garage. Should Patrick go inside? He'd wanted to talk to Mel alone, but it didn't seem that was going to happen.

After slamming the truck door, he rounded the hood of his truck and headed up the driveway. Luke was out of his vehicle by now and waved to him.

"Looking for Mel?" he asked Patrick.

"Yeah."

"I thought she was going to that board-of-education meeting tonight. She said she'd heard talk in town that it was going to be a big deal for you, and she hoped to offer you moral support. She wasn't there?"

Luke frowned, worried. Patrick didn't want him needlessly apprehensive. "She showed up after it was over, and she may have seen me with Dana. She drove off as though she had seen us and didn't like it. I have to talk to her about it."

"Dana, huh." Luke pursed his lips in thought and shifted the thermos in his hand to get a better grip. "In that case, you'd better come in and wait her out."

Patrick followed Luke up the steps to the back door and into the tiny, cramped kitchen. He dreamed of better for the two of them, but Luke was barely pulling thirty-five thou as a relatively new state trooper, and the accounting firm Mel worked for paid meager wages.

Still, the house was nice enough, better even than the first house he and Jenny had bought. Luke and Mel were still young. Things would improve as they got older.

Then again, look what had happened with Annabelle. So maybe not.

"Had any supper?" Luke asked as he scrubbed up at the sink

"Yeah. Before the meeting. Good thing, because I don't have much of an appetite now."

"What did that? The meeting or Mel?"

"Equal partners, I'd say." Patrick pulled out a chair at the dinette table and sat down. He watched as Luke assembled a sandwich out of the cold cuts he found in the fridge. "I'm surprised that Mel allows bologna in the house."

"I bought it. She wouldn't have. That woman is obsessed with good nutrition. But she's a good cook, so who am I to complain? I'll take her cooking over a bologna sandwich anytime." The sandwich complete, Luke joined him at the table. "What's the latest about Dana? It's all I hear these days. Mel worrying about you getting in over your head."

"I don't understand."

"What? Why she worries?" Luke laid the sandwich down and took a sip of the milk he'd poured.

"Mel worries because she's Mel. I've dated before. What's so different now?"

"In my opinion, the kid." Another swallow of milk, and Luke added, "She's freaking because you're seeing a woman who has a three-year-old."

"Because she thinks what? That I'm going to marry Dana, and I'll be responsible for bringing up Kate? That's crazy. I'm not even dating Dana."

Luke didn't reply. Patrick could tell his son-in-law was weighing a response as he finished up his sandwich.

"Spill it. You've obviously got a theory going." Patrick shifted on the dinette chair and wished for something to occupy his hands.

"Mel might say she was worried about you taking on that responsibility now, but that's not really what's at the root." Luke rose from the table to carry his plate to the dishwasher. It settled with a clink against the rack. He closed the dishwasher door before speaking. "You know I want kids, right?"

The question came so far out of left field that Patrick could only respond with, "Huh?"

"Kids. I want 'em. It'd be hard now, but I figure Mel and I could make it. We're not getting any younger."

"What's this have to do with Dana?"

Luke sat down again and nursed his glass of milk. When he did speak, he didn't answer Patrick's question. "Mel doesn't. Want kids, I mean. She says she doesn't want kids now. That we're not at a good spot, that we can't afford them. You know the drill."

Patrick laughed. "If you wait until you can afford kids, you'll never have them."

"Exactly. That's what I say. At first I thought Mel was just being Mel, all cautious and prepared, that that was holding her back."

"But you don't now?" Patrick wondered if Luke was simply exploiting the opportunity to vent while Mel wasn't here.

"Yeah. To me, it all goes back to the way Mel lost her little sister."

Luke's observation sucker punched Patrick in his gut. He was glad he was sitting down, but even so he had to steady himself with a hand on the table. "You think Mel doesn't want kids because of Annabelle?"

"I don't think. I know. And you do, too." Luke leaned forward, warming to his subject. "She has as little to do with her half brother as she can get by with. She steers clear of any kids in my family. She's the one who freaks if she runs out of birth control. Me? If we wind up expecting, no big deal. I figure it'll be great. Mel? She's one day late and she's pulling out the pregnancy tests as if the future of the world depends on it."

"I didn't know." Patrick rubbed at his jaw. This was one conversation he didn't want to be having. He cast a backward glance at the door, willing it to open. Even facing Mel's ire would be preferable to discussing pregnancy tests with his son-in-law.

"You're pulling my leg. Of course you knew. You

had to. Especially after Dana and Kate arrived on the scene and Mel started acting so weird."

"Why did that make you believe Mel doesn't want kids?"

Luke raised an eyebrow and drained his glass, then set it on the table with a thud. "I know Mel doesn't want kids. If she wanted them, she would have them, and nothing could stop her."

"Okay, then, why do you feel it's got something to do with Annabelle? Maybe Mel is just one of those women who, for whatever reason, doesn't want kids. Some women don't, Luke. You guys didn't talk about this before you got married?" Patrick was addressing Luke's back, because his son-in-law had gotten up to refresh his glass of milk.

"Of course we talked about it. We agreed that we'd wait." Luke poured his milk, stuck the carton back in the fridge and then kicked the door shut with his heel. "But we've waited five years. And she's not any less phobic on the subject now than she was when we tied the knot. How is it you can be so smart and not have seen that?"

"Seen what?" Patrick fiddled with one of the cork-backed coasters stacked on the table.

Luke snorted. "She practically hyperventilates at the prospect of you marrying Dana and becoming a father to Kate."

"Who says anything about me marrying Dana? I haven't even had the chance to ask the woman out for dinner and everybody seems to consider the wedding invitations ordered."

"Mel does, that's for sure. You don't hear her, sir. You don't hear her screaming at Lissa that Lissa's going to ruin your life by shoving you and Dana together. You don't hear her discuss and discuss and discuss how wrong a woman with a kid is for you. And God forbid I knock any of those objections of hers down with a good dose of common sense. She goes ballistic."

Patrick couldn't handle much more of this. He dropped the coaster and rose on legs that weighed two tons. "I'm sorry, Luke. I sure wish I knew what to say. But at least I know how strongly Mel feels about this now. If she'd just told me."

What? I wouldn't have allowed myself to be attracted to Dana? I've tried to put the boot to that, for all the good it's done.

He didn't want to hear one more reason he shouldn't pursue this thing with Dana. For once, he wanted to ignore the clear signs that he shouldn't do something.

"You're not going to wait for Mel?" Luke asked.

"What's the point?" Now, in addition to knowing that Mel would likely never be reconciled with any relationship he had with Dana, he had something else nagging at him. Could Luke be right? Had Annabelle's death screwed up Mel to the point that she didn't want kids? Or was it a personal choice of hers that had nothing to do with the past?

Were he a drinking man, he'd go home and get plastered. Instead, he decided, he'd just go home.

Patrick had made it to his truck, when Mel's car turned in the driveway. Fantastic. Talk about perfect timing.

She stalked toward him, her heels echoing on the concrete. "How could you? How could you lie about her?"

CHAPTER TWENTY-THREE

PATRICK HELD UP BOTH hands to ward off her anger. "I didn't lie, Mel. I seem to recall asking you what the problem was if I did date Dana."

"And *I* seem to recall explaining in minute detail why it was a problem. I thought you understood. Dad! Get a grip! You want to date? Fine. There are plenty of other women out there, women who don't have kids they are looking for you to rescue."

He leaned against the body of the truck and wished he hadn't bothered coming here at all. "That's not what Dana's about."

"Right." Mel rolled her eyes. "A single mom who's hit the gravy train for sure. Kids are trouble, Dad."

"Trouble?" Behind Mel, he saw Luke's shape through the kitchen window. It brought back Luke's insistence that Mel didn't want kids because of Annabelle. "What kind of trouble?"

"I can't believe that you of all people—" But Mel broke off. She folded her arms and stared at the tips of her shoes. "Kids are trouble. Your life isn't your own after you have a child. You know that. Even if everything turns out, you have to worry about them forever. Can't you just agree? Or do I have to go through an entire list of reasons that they're trouble?"

"You weren't." Suddenly weary, he opened the door of his truck and sagged against the seat.

"You're seriously considering this, then? What I saw tonight, you two in that truck—"

"Mel, honestly, this is between me and Dana. Whether we can work out a relationship or we can't, it's our business."

She closed in on him. "No, Dad, it's not just your business. It affects our entire family. Just like when Mom and Harrison decided, 'Gee whiz, it will be great shakes to have a baby.'"

Patrick latched on to that remark and couldn't let it go. He propped his hand on the door frame and sighed. "Kate is the heart of this issue, isn't she?"

"Not Kate in particular. Any baby. Any child." Now his daughter was avoiding his gaze again, staring straight down.

"Mel…" He drew in a breath. "Does this have anything to do with Annabelle?"

A siren pierced the air, inciting a volley of barking from the neighborhood dogs. Mel didn't look up from studying her shoes to answer his question.

Her response to it came too late to be convincing. "No. Of course not. It's to do with common sense."

"Listen, honey," he said as gently as he could manage. "I'm not forgetting Annabelle, okay? I think about her every day. But I can't say no to the possibility of a relationship with a woman just because she has a child."

"I see it, Dad. I see it in your eyes, how much it hurts you to be around children. Lissa doesn't care. She was too young to remember how losing Annabelle hurt you. But I wasn't. I saw it then and I see it now. Lissa believes kids are interchangeable. Like puppies or goldfish." Her mouth twisted. "Lose one?

Oh, just go get another. That worked for Mom when she had Christopher, so it should work for you, too, right? But it doesn't, and you know it—or you should, at least."

Patrick reached up and touched Mel's shoulder. She was shivering, whether from the cold or her emotions, he wasn't sure. "You don't have to tell me that. I know. Nobody's ever going to replace Annabelle."

She jerked away. "Then why try? Why put yourself through this agony?"

"I'm not trying to replace Annabelle. Not with Kate. Not with anybody. I'm just trying to move ahead. To get past this."

"You're trying to forget her."

"No. No."

"You promised me when we lost her that we'd never, ever forget her. That she'd always be with us." Tears streaked down Mel's face. "That's why you couldn't stay with Mom, because she *wanted* to forget her."

"Mel." Patrick massaged the ache in his temples. "I couldn't stay with your mother for a lot reasons. And yes, most of them had to do with Annabelle's death. But the marriage just wasn't meant to be."

"Not only Annabelle died then. Our whole family did, Dad. Everything. All of it gone. Nothing was the same afterward. Nothing could *ever* be the same."

"I realize that. But that doesn't mean we can't find happiness. It's not wrong to look, Mel. There's nothing wrong with attempting to make the best of what we have left. If Annabelle could tell us what she wanted, she'd say she wanted us to be happy." An odd sense of déjà vu swept over Patrick. When had he spoken these words? When had he had this conversation?

He hadn't. Or, rather, he had, but with Jenny uttering

the words. They'd been her sermon to him all those years ago when she'd told him she was leaving, and then later when she told him she and Harrison were expecting Christopher.

"Yeah. Mom and her pursuit of happiness." Mel's eyes flashed with anger. "She's moved on. She's past Annabelle's death. As if it never happened. Just like *you* want to move past it. That's what you said. Well, go on. Make a new happy little family with this Dana and her kid. And forget us. Forget we ever existed."

Mel spun on her heel and ran for the house.

Dana grabbed the phone on the first ring so that it wouldn't wake up Kate. "Hello?"

"Dana? It's Patrick. Look, I know it's late. But can I stop by?"

She turned her back to Lissa, who was gathering her things up from the kitchen table. "Uh, sure. What's the matter?"

"Blowup with Mel. I'd rather talk about it in person. See you in five."

With that he hung up, and Dana replaced the handset. She considered whether to say anything to Lissa.

Lissa beat her to the punch. "I just got an 'I hate you. I hope you're satisfied' text from Mel. And that sounded like Dad on the phone. So let me guess. He's coming over here because Mel caught you two together."

"Something like that."

"Honestly, my sister needs professional help." Her books stacked together, her iPod in its case, Lissa swung her purse onto her shoulder. "If she could just get over herself and let you have a chance. But she's so paranoid that when I tell her that, she insists it's just me driving a wedge between her and Dad."

Lissa was out the door on a blast of cold air before Dana could reply.

Dana watched through the kitchen window as Patrick talked with Lissa on his way. Lissa's hands, despite her load of books, were going wild with her gesticulations. Dana even spotted a stamped foot. The conversation didn't last long.

Patrick headed for the door, and Dana had it open before he made it to the top of her back steps. "I'm sorry, Patrick."

"For what? Giving me a curl-up-the-toes kiss?" He walked inside, past Dana. Despite the unruffled demeanor he projected, she noticed he didn't offer up any more of those kisses.

Dana shut the door and leaned against it. "For upsetting Mel." Dana couldn't shake the queasy sensation that she'd broken something of Patrick's that would prove to be irreplaceable. Hadn't Jenny warned her about this?

Now she turned back to Patrick, who stood in the center of the kitchen, his earlier certainty not so evident. He frowned. "Mel," he repeated.

"Lissa said Mel was steamed."

"I'd have to agree. For once, Lissa isn't exaggerating."

From the rear of the house, Dana heard a plaintive, "Mommy?"

"Hold on. Let me check on Kate," she told him.

"Sorry. I didn't mean to wake her."

Dana didn't realize he'd followed her to Kate's room until she was almost at the end of the hall. Before she could gesture for him to stay back, she saw Kate stir from her cocoon of pink sheets. "I'm thirsty, Mommy."

"I'll get her a glass of water," Patrick volunteered.

Dana perched on the side of the bed and smoothed the sheets. "It's late, sweetie. You need to go to sleep," she told Kate.

"But you're still up. And Mr. Patrick's here." A yawn interrupted her argument.

"Shh. You'll wake up Rascal." Dana nodded at the dog, who was curled in a knot on the floor. "Mr. Patrick's about to go home and go to bed." *Alone. Without me. Which is exactly how it should be, and forget any toe-curling kisses.*

Patrick reappeared with the glass of water. Kate struggled up and wrapped both hands around the glass.

"What do you tell him?"

"Thank you, Mr. Patrick." The gratitude obediently expressed, Kate gulped the water.

"Easy. Not too much."

"Mommy, I think I'm gonna have a bad dream."

"No, no, you're not. It's okay. Go to sleep, all right."

"But I'm *scared*, Mommy!" Kate wailed.

Patrick knelt beside the bed and took the water from Kate. "Who's that brave girl who helped her mom get those thorns out of my hand?"

Kate sniffled. "Me. Is your boo-boo better?"

Patrick produced the hand for her inspection. "It is. See? You were brave then, a lot braver than me. You're going to be okay. You've got all these animals here to keep you company. And Rascal."

Her blue eyes filled with doubt. She gripped her doll and put stranglehold on her giraffe. "But I'm scared."

"No bad dreams tonight," Patrick assured her. "I know. You know how I know?"

Kate shook her head.

"Because I know a song that will help you think of something else. I used to sing it to my little girl."

Dana held her breath as Patrick placed Kate's hand

in his and began crooning a lullaby. It was a crazy silly one, a song that she suspected Patrick had made up out of whole cloth years earlier. Kate giggled at the nonsense of it, then yawned again, then giggled, then with one final yawn closed her eyes.

Patrick and Dana crept to the door, only to be stopped by another drowsy question.

"Mr. Patrick?"

"Yes, Kate?"

"Do you want another little girl?"

Patrick froze beside Dana. His face showed bewildered panic, as if Kate had just asked him to breathe under water. Dana didn't wait for him to tussle with a response. She turned back to Kate and gave her one final pat.

"Baby girl, you're my angel. Don't you offer to be anybody else's baby girl." Dana pressed a kiss to Kate's forehead. "Now, go to sleep. No more stalling."

This time, Dana and Patrick made it all the way along the hall and to the living room. Patrick's exhalation of relief was audible.

"Sorry."

"No problem." Patrick dropped onto the couch and twirled the glass of water in his hands. "Will she hear us in here?"

"She's down for the count now." Where to sit? Next to him on the couch? In the chair? She stayed put, studying his face under the light from the lamp.

"Mel used to drive me crazy when she was little. I'd have to check under the bed, behind the curtains, in the closet."

"Sounds like she's still driving you crazy." Maybe the remark wasn't as subtle as it should have been, but Dana couldn't help herself. She wanted to know about the conversation between Mel and him.

"You can say that again." Patrick patted the sofa. "Come sit."

She sank down beside him, conscious of how close he was and how different things felt now between them. "Want to talk about it?"

"I've screwed up, Dana."

CHAPTER TWENTY-FOUR

AT HIS WORDS, Dana clenched her hand on her knee. She'd known this was what he'd come by to say. Whom had she been kidding? If there was a choice to be made, of course he would choose his family. As he should.

"How?" Might as well get it over and done with.

"Mel thinks the Connors can't be happy, that we don't deserve happiness, after losing Annabelle."

This wasn't what Dana had expected. She relaxed her hand, spread it palm-flat on her knee. Patrick reached out and laid his fingers over hers.

"But she can't think that, not really, Patrick."

"Why not? I have. Maybe not consciously, but I realized that I did. Tonight. I was having the same argument with Mel I'd had all those years ago with Jenny, only this time, Mel was me and I…I was Jenny."

Dana peeked at him. His face was drawn and he was absorbed in thought, but he didn't appear tortured. "What changed your mind?"

"You. And, yeah, I have to admit it, being around Kate. It's nuts, but I had to be around her to realize she wasn't Annabelle. For the first time, I see how crazy I drove Jenny."

"But what about Mel?"

"I don't know. I honestly don't know." He let his head loll on the back of the sofa and stared up at the ceiling. "I feel that if I pursue this chance I have with you, then I lose what I have with Mel."

"You can't jeopardize your relationship with your daughter, Patrick." The words had been clogging in her throat, but Dana got them out. Yet, it wasn't fair. He was finally getting unstuck and now Mel was holding him back.

"Lissa swears that Mel will get over this." He shook his head. Dana could tell he was struggling to convince himself.

"But you don't believe that."

"I want to." He lifted his head and took Dana's hands in his. "You know that, don't you?"

"Sure."

"But I'm not certain I can buy into Lissa's optimism. I want to believe it. I mean, hell, I haven't even invited you out for the requisite dinner and a movie."

She was disappointed enough to refuse to bow out gracefully. "Why me? Why am I different? You've dated lots of women—at least, according to Lissa—and Mel hasn't had a problem with them."

"Kate."

"Kate's not going away. She and I are a package deal."

"I realize that."

They sat in silence. Dana wished for the moment back in Patrick's truck, where she'd forgotten all the reasons she and Patrick wouldn't work.

"We're just doomed, aren't we? If we're not ticking each other off, we've got all this other baggage to contend with." She should say goodbye to him, walk him to the door, out of her life, and do her damnedest to fall for somebody like Vann. So why wouldn't her legs cooperate?

Her words seemed to galvanize him. "No. We are not doomed. I'm inviting you out for that dinner. What are you doing Saturday night?"

"Wait, Patrick. Is this wise?"

"It's dinner. That's all."

"We shouldn't. What happens when ultimately you're forced to choose? It may not happen now. It may happen later on down the road, when Kate's gotten to know you and grown attached." *When I've grown attached.*

"For once, let's live with reckless abandon. Go to dinner. Not consider tomorrow. Hmm?" He cupped her face in his hands and touched his nose to hers. "I could kiss you until you said yes, but I'd rather know your yes was not the result of undue influence. I've had a hell of a night tonight. Don't let your no be the cherry on top."

I'm going to regret this. "Who would I get to babysit Kate?"

"Lissa, of course."

Dana tried to pull back out of Patrick's hold on her. "I don't know. Mel won't like it. It'll just cause more friction between her and Lissa."

"Leave Mel and Lissa to me. Come to dinner."

"Well…"

"Unless you've got something you have to do Saturday."

"Overdue Christmas shopping in Savannah. Being Santa when you're a single parent is hard."

For a moment, she thought that was that. He'd gone still on her, almost frozen, his hold on her hand loosening. She knew from his faraway expression that he was thinking of playing Santa for Annabelle.

"Hey, Patrick, no big deal. Maybe some other time, okay?" She tugged her hand from his and patted him.

"No." His answer was firm. He looked more like a man

saying yes to an IRS audit than to a date. "I'll drive you to Savannah and we'll be Santa together. And have dinner."

Against her better judgment, she nodded. "If you're sure. But if you change your mind, I'll understand."

PATRICK DIDN'T change his mind, but Dana nearly did. She got within an inch of pulling the plug on all of it, when Mel showed up on her doorstep.

Dana stood in the doorway and gaped in amazement at Patrick's daughter.

"Mel. Are you hunting for your dad?"

"Lissa."

"She's in the kitchen. Come in." Dana gestured for Mel to follow her.

Lissa was preparing Kate's lunch plate, her back to the door. She spoke to Dana without turning around. "You've got fifteen minutes before Dad gets here, and trust me, you don't want to be late."

"Lissa. Mel's here to see you."

Little sister faced big sister. Lissa frowned. "What do you want?"

Mel folded her arms and compressed her lips. "You said you'd help me with sorting out stuff at Dad's for the charity auction. Was that before or after you agreed to babysit so Dad could go out on a date?"

Lissa groaned. She set Kate's plate on the counter. "Oh, Mel, I completely forgot."

"What's new?" The hurt in Mel's eyes belied her blasé tone. "Forget it. You weren't going to help, anyway. I'll do it myself."

"No! I said I would. I mean, I can babysit Kate at Dad's as easily as I can babysit her here. It will be okay, won't it, Dana? Me taking Kate to Dad's?"

Dana started to voice her hesitation, but didn't get the chance. Mel pivoted on her heel and said over her shoulder, "No. I don't want Kate at Dad's. It's fine. I'll do it by myself."

Mel's snippiness rubbed Dana the wrong way. "It's fine with me," Dana said. "But I'd ask your dad if he has a problem with it."

The split second of disappointment in Mel's eyes revealed the girl's frustration at things not turning out as she'd wanted them to. Dana realized that Mel had hoped to guilt-trip Lissa into not watching Kate.

And then boom, Dana wouldn't be able to go to Savannah with Patrick.

He was wrong. Mel wasn't going to get over this. She was jealous of Dana, or at least of the potential Dana had to be a serious rival for Patrick's affection.

Lissa was on the phone with Patrick, explaining the situation. While Lissa apparently received a "You should write things down and keep your promises" lecture, Mel and Dana eyed another.

Dana blinked first. Who was she to appear and drive a wedge between father and daughter?

To cover her thoughts, she called Kate in to the kitchen and put her plate on the table. Dana felt Mel's eyes on her and Kate.

"So you and Dad are going to Savannah?"

"For the day."

Mel's eyebrows shot up. "Of course. For the day." Her fingers dug into the fabric of her jacket. "What are your plans?"

"Christmas shopping."

The skin around Mel's eyes tightened, but her smile never faltered. Dana decided that having someone who hated you so much pretend to be nice to you was eerie.

"Okay, then," Lissa interrupted. "Dad says it's fine with him. So, Kate, how do you feel about a treasure hunt? We're going to help Mel find treasure!"

Mel's knuckles went white. She glanced at Kate, then Dana, then out the kitchen window. "Yeah. Like we're going to get a lot accomplished babysitting," she muttered.

"Oh, and Dad said he was just about here, so you'd better hustle." This last bit advice from Lissa was to Dana.

Dana hesitated. "Maybe I shouldn't go."

Mel brightened at the prospect, but Lissa crossed the kitchen and gently shoved Dana toward the door. "Go. When else will you help Santa? It will be a nightmare this close to Christmas."

Dana saw Mel's face pale. "Dad is going Christmas shopping for—" She swallowed, her throat moving visibly. "Lissa!"

Patrick banged on the back door.

"Go! I'll stall him!" Lissa grinned and pushed at Dana again.

I shouldn't be doing this.

Then Patrick was entering though the back door. Kate ran to greet him; Lissa shouted out a greeting. Cacophony. For a moment, Dana allowed herself to be swept away in the fantasy that this could be her life.

She let herself be urged out of the room on that wave of wishful thinking, only to be caught short by Mel's glower. Oh, yeah. Exactly the sort of life she wanted to have.

PATRICK WAS HALFWAY down the driveway when he realized Dana wasn't behind him. Instead, she stood at the top of the steps, one hand clutching her purse, the other still gripping the doorknob.

He backtracked. "Hey. Forget something?"

She didn't take her eyes off the window in the door. "Maybe I shouldn't come."

"What?" Well, this was a development he hadn't considered. He'd figured he was the one most likely to wig out and run screaming from Toys "R" Us. In fact, if they dawdled much longer, he might lose his nerve completely.

"I just don't feel right about leaving."

"You don't trust Lissa?" Patrick scrutinized how she still hadn't let go of the doorknob. "Or you just don't want to go?"

Dana narrowed her eyes. "Now you're putting words in my mouth."

"You've left Kate with Lissa lots of times," he went on, not answering her question.

"Yeah, to go to the pool for an hour. This is different. I'll be gone all day."

"Look, if you don't want to come, don't." Patrick hated that he sounded as churlish and disappointed as a ten-year-old boy. "But I had a surprise planned for us."

Now her fingers relaxed a fraction. "A surprise?"

"Yeah."

"What sort of surprise?"

"If I told you, it wouldn't be a surprise, would it?"

She sighed and glanced back through the window. "Maybe it's because of Mel. I didn't feel any hesitation until she showed up."

Patrick grasped her by the shoulders. "Maybe this is a good thing, Dana. Mel will be forced to spend some time with Kate and Lissa, and she'll realize you and me together isn't the worst thing in the world."

"The way you did?"

Had he realized that? If he had, then why was he trying not to think about Christmas shopping for a toddler?

"Yeah," he lied. "The way I did."

CHAPTER TWENTY-FIVE

PATRICK WEDGED the cart in between a grandfather and a mom bent on buying out the store. How anyone could afford as much merchandise as this woman had heaped in her cart, he couldn't comprehend. But then, hadn't he spent more than he should have on Annabelle?

Dana had slid past the grandpa and the mom and was now scanning the shelves for some hot toy that Kate had on her wish list.

So far so good. That the store was packed with desperate crazy parents and management had elected to pipe in Christmas carols at ear-popping decibels helped. You couldn't think. You couldn't concentrate. You didn't remember past shopping trips for a family who didn't exist anymore.

As long as he didn't see anything pink. Or ballet inspired. Or with princesses.

Which pretty much wiped out any shopping in the girls' section, so maybe it *was* a good thing Gramps was blocking his path to Dana.

His escape route cut off by the trio of women behind him debating the moral implications of buying Bratz dolls, Patrick leaned against shelves loaded with fluffy stuffed animals that came in their own pet carriers. He'd made the mistake of elbowing one. It still hadn't stopped yowling its fifty different electronic messages.

Of course the damn thing had to be pink.

The wagon train ahead of him inched forward. He moved up as much as he could before being blocked again. Now he was closer to Dana, firmly in the dress-up section. Feather boas tickled his nose and attire fit for the most finicky princess hung from the shelves.

Am I pwetty, Daddy? Do you wike the pink one or the purple one?

He gritted his teeth at the memory, gripped the cart in the hope that he wouldn't run like a man on fire from this store.

"Patrick?" Dana tapped him on the arm. "You okay?"

"Sure. Fine. A headache," he lied. "All this noise."

"It is loud in here." Dana stared at him. "Do we need to go?"

"No. Of course not. What's that?" He gestured toward the shiny rhinestone-encrusted pink satin in Dana's hand.

"A complete princess dress-up kit. Actually, a yard of cheap satin sewed onto a tube top. If I could sew worth anything, I could run this up on a sewing machine and be fifty bucks ahead. As it is…"

"Cheaper to buy it?"

"Easier. Next year I swear I'm doing all my shopping online."

It was what she wasn't saying that Patrick heard. And that was clear from her concentration on Patrick. She watched him with as much diligence as she would a ticking time bomb.

That's me. A ticking time bomb.

Or was that Mel? He'd been astonished to find her at Dana's this morning. When he'd attempted to talk to Mel about this trip, Mel had refused to listen. She'd just kept saying he was trying to replace the family they'd had, trying to forget.

Exactly what he'd accused Jenny of. He'd said as much to Mel, but that had simply incensed her more. Her reaction scared him. Had he been the kind of father who'd crippled his daughter? Had he really pounded into her head that sacrificing future happiness was required in order to honor Annabelle's memory?

For him to make that sacrifice was okay. But Mel was young. She had her whole life in front of her.

So Patrick had decided then and there that he'd muscle through this. Dana wanted to go Christmas shopping? Fine. He'd do it, if that was what he needed to do to show Mel having a life was permissible.

Only, he hadn't realized how hard this trip would be.

"Hey." Dana closed her hand over his arm, touched his face. "This is too much. Let's go."

"No." He shook her off. "I said I'm fine, and I am. What's next on your list?"

Dana puckered her brow but didn't attempt to touch him again. "You don't look fine. But it's your call."

They pushed ahead, the store closing in on Patrick. Everything he saw—the big stuffed bear, the pretend makeup, the baby dolls—slammed him back into another life.

He'd been alone the last time he shopped for Annabelle. He remembered how he'd arrived home and started to work on assembling a bike, a two-wheeler with training wheels.

"She's not big enough to ride that, Patrick. Why on earth did you buy it? She can't even ride a trike."

"Jenny, you've got to have faith. She'll get better. She did before. This treatment's going to work, and she'll go into remission and she'll come home. She's going to

*come home. She'll ride this. See? It's got training
wheels—"*

*"She's not getting better. She's not. And you're so
far in denial that you're putting together a bike that
she's never going to ride."*

Jenny had been right. Annabelle hadn't ever ridden
it. He still had that bike, with its pink tassels and its little
bell and the wire basket on the front.

Dana and he were in the baby doll section now. He
was surrounded by pink-cheeked babies who wet and
pooped and ate and cried, "Mama." Why didn't toy
makers ever make a doll that cried, "Daddy?"

His gaze fell on a doll designed to be sick—Nurse-
me-Mommy, it was called. Complete with a thermome-
ter and a toy stethoscope and pretend medicine to make
the fever go down.

Twisted. Toy manufacturers were twisted. Why the
hell would they ever think playing at treating a sick baby
was a good thing? Why help kids believe that a few
droppers full of medicine was all it took to make a baby
well?

Patrick didn't even realize he was running until he
was out the doors of the store and into the mall. He
couldn't breathe, couldn't speak; his heart was
pounding as though he'd sprinted miles. He leaned
forward, propped his hands on his knees.

"Patrick?" Now Dana was beside him, guiding him
to a bench by the fountain. "What happened?"

"God, I don't know. Did you see that Nurse-me-
Mommy doll? How sick is that?" Which sounded crazy.
He sounded crazy.

"This wasn't such a good idea, was it?" Dana's
dispirited tone told him she wasn't talking about the
doll.

"No. I mean, yes. Hell. I don't know. I'll be okay."

He couldn't meet her eyes. What if he saw in them how nuts she must think he was?

"Tell you what. You stay put. I'll go check out. I'm done, anyway."

He'd read her list. She was nowhere near done, but he was pathetically grateful not to have to return to that torture chamber. He watched her go. If he were with her, he'd have this to do every year. Every birthday. And Valentine's Day. And Easter. And for any of the other thousands of reasons retailers dreamed up to sell toys.

Patrick rose on shaky legs and gazed at the people milling around the mall. At that couple holding hands, who must be dating. And the mom with the stroller, kneeling to tease her baby. That group of teenagers, traveling in a pack.

They all looked happy. All looked as though they had their lives together, that nothing bad had happened to them.

Come to think of it, Dana had that happy, untouched-by-the-travails-of-life look—at least she did before he'd backslid into a panic attack.

But would she keep her happiness if he couldn't manage simple things like Christmas shopping?

Nearby, a girl of about eight stood with a man who was probably her dad. The guy kept glancing back in to the toy store. Patrick knew the score. Mom was inside buying Christmas presents, and Dad was responsible for making sure she didn't get busted. The guy was handing his daughter a penny.

The child tossed it, and the copper disc sailed into the air before it landing with a *plink* in the fountain. From her disappointed expression, it had landed on tails.

What had she wished for?

He pulled out a handful of change. Fingered a penny. What would he wish for? Something he knew would come true? Or something impossible, something beyond reason?

"If I go to heaven, will you go wif me?"

"No, baby, it's not like that. The Lord decides who gets to go first."

"You want me to hold your place in line, Daddy? I will. I'll let you cut in."

The penny felt warm in his hand from gripping the coin so tightly. How panicked he was at this moment, how afraid he'd somehow make the wrong wish. Wishes didn't come true. Prayers didn't.

Patrick opened his hand and stared down at the penny. The date of issue on its reddish-brown surface was the year Annabelle had died.

Had his life ground to a standstill that year? Had Jenny been right in saying that he could move on if he could just get over this guilt?

Mel's words returned to mind. She'd said their family had died that year. No arguing there. And it had died because of one choice he'd made.

Patrick looked from the penny back into the store, where Dana stood at the checkout. She was handing the cashier the princess outfit.

Heads, I have permission to move on. Not to forget, but to live.

He tossed the penny. It sailed high into the air, flipping once, twice, on its way down. Then it hit the water in the fountain and sank to the black bottom. He leaned forward.

The penny had landed on tails.

DANA KICKED HERSELF for not realizing how hard this would be on Patrick. She shouldn't have gotten involved with a guy with so much baggage. She wasn't equipped.

Palm out, she waited for the clerk to hand her the credit card slip to sign. The woman patted her apron, looked on the cash register and frowned. "I can't find my pen."

Dana jerked her attention back from Patrick, who was staring into the fountain. "Your ear," she told the clerk.

The woman's face split into a grin. Embarrassed, she yanked the pen from where it was tucked behind her ear and handed it to Dana. "Always the last place you look," she said.

Dana scrawled her signature on the slip and shoved it toward the cashier.

"That your husband?" The woman was taking her sweet time separating the slips and handing back the yellow customer's copy. "I saw you and him run out— saw you park your cart over there. He sick?"

Dana glanced out at Patrick, standing were she'd left him. "He's okay." Was that a lie or wishful thinking? She held out her hand for the receipt that still hadn't crossed from the cashier's palm to hers. "Thank you." Dana hoped the nicety would prompt the woman.

It didn't; however, the throat-clearing in the line behind Dana did. She grabbed her bags and headed for Patrick.

"Done?"

Patrick's face was more relaxed now, his frown gone. The minutes outside the toy store had apparently given him time to calm down.

"I'm sorry, Patrick."

"It's okay. Ready for your surprise? Or do you still have some more shopping?"

Was the tone of that last question shaky? Or was her imagination overvigilant?

"I'm calling the shopping quits for today." She was sure she saw tension ease from his shoulders.

"Great." His eyes locked on to the penny-covered bottom of the fountain for a long moment. He exhaled, shook his head as if to clear it and grabbed the biggest bag she carried. "Let's get out of here."

CHAPTER TWENTY-SIX

DANA ABSORBED the seedy surroundings flashing by the car windows and attempted to quell her nervousness. "Uh, this is not such a great neighborhood," she commented.

"I know." Patrick didn't glance her way. He kept driving. "It gets better. You're not familiar with this section of Savannah?"

"Never put so much as my pinkie toe in this area. Why? What's my surprise if it's here?"

"Wait and see." He made a right turn, then hooked a left. Dana noticed the run-down houses gave way to a spit of land jutting out into water. A big, white-shingled structure stood at the end of it. The wooden sign hanging drunkenly askew proclaimed the place, The Shellcove Yacht Club."

"I had no idea this was even here."

"Welcome to the best-kept-secret yacht club in Savannah. This is where the real fishermen keep their boats."

"You have a boat?" Her mouth dropped open.

"Nah, not me. Can't afford the upkeep. But I did some work for a guy who can afford it, and he lets me use his boat on occasion. I phoned ahead and asked if we could sail it down river for lunch."

Dana leaned forward as the truck crunched over the oyster-shell parking lot. "This is my surprise?"

"Are you disappointed? You don't get seasick, do you?" He pulled into a parking space close to the dock.

"No. Well, I don't know. I don't guess I get seasick. Wow. This is… I lived in Savannah for ten years and no one ever took me out on the water."

"Not even Mr. 'You can sue—I can help?'" He quirked an eyebrow.

"Oh, no. He was much too busy chasing ambulances and buxom brunettes. What sort of boat does your friend have?"

"Now, don't get too excited. It's no Onassis yacht, okay?"

But it was big enough to have a small cabin tucked under the deck. Dana surveyed the tiny space, complete with a two-burner cooktop and a microscopic fridge and microwave. The cooktop held a big, cast-iron Dutch oven.

Patrick lifted the lid on the pot, and the rich briny scent of shrimp floated on the air. "Yeah, they put our lunch in here. Now all we have to do is head out."

The air smelled marshy as Patrick eased the vessel out of the slip and directed the boat into the open waterway. "I can't believe you lived in Savannah as long as you did and you never went out on a boat," he shouted over the roar of the engine.

"Not my crowd," she said. "Besides, by the time I worked my shifts at the hospital, I didn't have much of a social life. Why do you think I wound up falling for an ambulance chaser?"

"Want to try your hand at steering?"

"Me? I'd wreck the boat!"

"No, you won't. Here." He pulled her into the shelter of his arms, placed her hands on the controls. "Go on."

For an exhilarating few minutes, she felt the power

of the craft under her hands. She looked up at Patrick. "This is great! Wow!"

"I had to do something spectacular. I waited too long for the stale old dinner and a movie."

She suppressed the worrisome thought that perhaps he'd brought other women here. Why let it bother her? His history of dating—not to mention his reaction at the toy store—made it abundantly clear that he wouldn't be around for the long haul. But for now she could pretend that she was something special.

"All right, there are some tricky spots ahead. I'd better take the wheel again, find us a spot where we can park this sucker. All set for lunch?"

"Is it lunchtime already?" she asked him.

Patrick pressed his lips to hers in a quick kiss that took her completely by surprise. "That's because you were so charmingly disappointed at the idea that this ride might be over. I intend to have a long, long lunch with you."

She laughed. "Had to conspire to get me on a boat in the middle of nowhere so you could have uninterrupted time?"

"Now you know my evil plan." Patrick waggled his eyebrows. The gesture sent a shiver of anticipation through her.

"Hmm, guess I'd better head for the galley and warm up that food, then. If you're going to catch me, you'd best keep your energy up." She disentangled herself from his embrace.

Down in the little galley, Dana gripped the counter and tried to accommodate for legs that quivered. The trembling had nothing to do with the water rolling gently beneath the boat and everything to do with the man who was topside.

Lunch was a low-country boil, full of pink shrimp,

fat sausages, corn and potatoes, which the yacht club's restaurant had put together.

Her heart thudded as she heard him coming down the ladder into the cabin.

Don't make a fool of yourself.

Patrick's complete lack of small talk over lunch did little to ease her apprehensions. The silence unnerved her.

That didn't stop her from craving Patrick. Every time he popped a shrimp into that delectable mouth of his, she couldn't help imagining the feel of his lips on her. She forced herself to look anywhere but his face, because each time she did, she couldn't look anywhere else.

What am I doing here? Dana asked herself.

"Thank you," she blurted in a desperate move to get her mind out of its endless loop of where the afternoon could lead.

Patrick paused in his eating, a bite of potato halfway to his mouth. "For lunch?"

"For everything. This, the boat, everything. Especially after this morning. After I finished up at the toy store I halfway expected you'd want to go back to Logan."

His fingers tightened on the fork and his mouth compressed. Patrick stared down at his plate. "I'm sorry I acted like such an idiot. I'd tell you why, except I don't know why. I thought I'd…"

He didn't finish, and she hoped Patrick had been going to say, *made a breakthrough.* But wasn't it too much to expect he could just decide to be okay, and bingo he would be? Dana swallowed. "You didn't act like an idiot. I was the idiot, asking you to do something that had to tear you apart. I should be the one—"

"Apologizing? Again?" Patrick's mouth twisted into a crooked smile that didn't reach his eyes. He set the fork down.

Dana covered his hand with hers. "Yes. Again. I didn't realize how hard shopping for children's toys would be, Patrick."

"Not a big deal." He squeezed her fingers. This time his smile was wider. Still, it didn't go beyond his lips.

"Let me guess. You don't want to talk about it." Dana pulled her hand back.

"I can talk about it. There's just nothing to say. I got in there. It was crowded. I saw some toy company's sick idea of entertainment, and I just had to have some air. That's all."

She grabbed up her dish and stood, then turned in the narrow galley to face the sink. With an aggressive squirt of detergent and a scrub brush, she attacked the plate.

"Hey." Patrick came up behind her, his breath on her nape. "What did I say?"

Dana rinsed the plate, concentrating on the water sluicing over it as she struggled to figure out her anger. With fingers steadier than how she felt, she dropped the rinsed plate into the dish drainer. "It's what you don't say, Patrick."

Now she reached for her glass, but Patrick stopped her with a hand on her arm. He swiveled her in his grasp. "What can I tell you? Words don't bring her back. They don't make me feel any better."

"What will?" She was conscious of his hands on her waist, his fingers warm through her blouse.

"You." Now one hand moved to her face. Patrick's fingers grazed her skin as his eyes locked with hers. "You make it better."

Dana settled her hands on his shoulders. "I didn't this morning."

"Forget about this morning." His lips dropped to her temple, skimmed along her skin. He tilted her mouth up to meet hers, and the moment that it did, she promptly lost all rational thought. She was conscious only of the counter biting into her back, the crispness of Patrick's shirt under her fingers, the tantalizing warmth of his mouth on hers.

She pressed against him, but he leaned her away from him. His lips nuzzled her throat, pushed aside her collar and trailed along the sensitive skin there. He fumbled with the blouse's buttons. The shirt fell open under his assault and his fingers smoothed down the hollow between her breasts. She gripped the counter at the vortex of sensation he was creating within her.

At her sharp intake of breath, Patrick stilled and held her eyes. The expression in them was a challenge, a dare.

She answered with every quivering molecule of her body. Now *her* fingers wrestled with buttons. Dana edged aside his shirt, her mouth following her fingers. His breath rasped as her lips found that sweet spot on his neck. Her tongue slid along it. Her teeth grazed it.

Patrick groaned and pulled away from her. His hands threaded into her hair and brought her mouth back to his. She and he became twined together again, each trying to get closer still to the other, skin to skin. Only her bra was between them.

They were moving now, and Dana couldn't have said who made the first step toward the tiny bedroom. When they got to the threshold of the little room, Patrick leaned her against the door frame. His lips found the curve of her breast, and she arched closer.

The boat rocked under them. Patrick let the bed catch them. They fell in a heap, limbs and lips tangled.

For a stretch of minutes, they satisfied themselves with kisses, each hungrier than the one before. Then Patrick sat up, letting the fingers of one hand trace her jawline as he reached for something with the other.

"What?" she murmured, weaving her fingers through his.

"Well…" He colored.

Dana looked past their interlaced hands to see that in his other he held his wallet. A coldness washed over her.

She knew the score. Marty had done this to her four years earlier—pulled a condom out of a wallet.

Kate was proof enough that the condom had failed.

And Dana had been about to put her faith in thin latex again. Back then, she'd thought, *Oh, well, if it doesn't hold, no big deal*.

But she knew better now. If her own husband wouldn't stay with her, no man who couldn't hack a toy store after the death of his daughter would stick around.

Dana struggled upright and yanked her blouse closed. She breathed a sigh of relief that she hadn't completely lost her mind.

"Huh?" Patrick appear confused.

"I'm sorry. I don't know what got into me." Her words came out husky. She couldn't face him. "I can't."

Water lapped against the hull of the boat. A Sea-Doo roared by. Then the sound faded and the water could be heard lapping again.

Patrick exhaled shakily. He stood, his back to her. "Okay. I thought— Well, it doesn't matter what I thought, does it? I'll take you home."

He strode down the length of the boat and grasped

the ladder to the deck. Halfway up, he paused as if about to say something. Dana held her breath, not sure if his reaction would be anger or hurt or disappointment.

But Patrick just muttered something and continued his climb, leaving Dana alone on the bed they might have shared.

CHAPTER TWENTY-SEVEN

THE DRIVE BACK was a tense, quiet one, and Dana could have sworn that Logan had moved fifty miles farther from Savannah since they'd left.

Patrick hadn't said two words between the time they'd arrived at the truck and he'd made the drive to the interstate. Overpasses and mile markers blipped by.

She'd tried. She'd apologized for leading him on. She'd made an effort to explain, but he'd cut her off with a curt, "Hey. Your perogative. You don't owe me anything. Can we just not talk about this?"

The moment had collapsed when she'd seen him reach for his wallet. He couldn't talk about his daughter. So how on earth would he be ready to stick around in case Dana got pregnant, Dana asked herself anew.

Still, she found cold comfort in knowing that she'd made the right decision. He sat behind the wheel, his fingers gripping it as though he wanted to choke it—or her.

She tried again. "Look, I'm sorry. What happened wasn't fair, I realize. But I just couldn't, Patrick."

Patrick glanced at her through slitted eyes, then turned back to the interstate ahead. "You were the one who wanted things simple."

A true statement, but still it stung. "I guess our definitions of *simple* don't match."

He lifted his eyebrows. "I guess not." Patrick resumed his close-mouthed driving, apparently deciding that he'd gotten—and wanted to keep—the last word.

She would not feel badly about this. Yes, she'd made a mistake, a miscalculation. But she'd done the right thing, and if he couldn't understand, so be it. Better for them to end the relationship now.

The ring of Dana's cell phone punctuated the tense silence in the car. She fumbled in her bag. Lissa. This would be an awkward conversation.

From the moment Dana heard Lissa's hiccuping sobs, however, all thought about what she'd been doing left her.

"Lissa? What's wrong?"

"Dana, you've got to believe it was an accident. You've got to."

"What's wrong? Where's Kate?"

"We were in the attic, you know, going through Dad's stuff for Goodwill, just like we said." More sniffles. "And Mel and I got to arguing. I wasn't paying attention—it was my fault."

"What? What's wrong with Kate? Tell me!" Panic had taken hold of her and the question was shrieked.

The truck swerved to the emergency lane, bumping along the speed breaks. Patrick slammed the transmission into park. He was facing Dana, his body rigid.

"The next thing we heard was a crash. She'd pulled this old TV off on top of her—I think she wanted a candy jar on top."

Dana screamed. She didn't know what she screamed, but she had visions of the children who'd brought dressers and televisions and bookshelves down on top of themselves and ended up in her E.R.

"No, no, she's not—she's alive. It wasn't a very big

television. But she's hurt—bad. I'm so sorry, so very sorry." Now Lissa was crying too much for Dana to understand anything, if she could have comprehended any words at this point.

Dana couldn't process any air. She inhaled huge gasps that did nothing to help her breathe. Patrick snatched the phone from her.

"Lissa, put Mel on. I need to talk to Mel."

A moment later, he must have heard Mel giving him an update, because he was repeating terrifying snatches of conversation. "Internal injuries…ruptured spleen…, uh-huh…concussion…surgery."

He glanced at Dana. Then he closed his eyes tightly and white-knuckled the steering wheel. "Mel. Listen. Get hold of yourself. Get hold of Lissa. We're on our way." His voice was deadly calm. "I want you to call Jenny. You tell her what you told me. No. Call her. Now. Tell her…tell her I said I need her to be there. Ask her about this doctor."

He snapped the phone shut and tossed it on the seat. Then he jerked the truck into gear and turned on the flashers. Dana heard a screech as the tires burned rubber on the roadway.

Dana's right hand tightened on the grip handle above her door. Her other hand maintained its viselike hold on the seat as Patrick sped up the interstate and began weaving in and out of traffic.

"Say again what kind of injuries," she ordered.

"They don't know everything. Some fractured ribs, a collapsed lung, a concussion. They think she's got a ruptured spleen. They don't want to move her to Macon, though—just get her into surgery ASAP. That's why I told Mel to get Jenny there."

Dana couldn't wrap her head around that. "Why Jenny?"

Patrick shot Dana a bewildered look. "She's a doctor. Didn't you know that? If anybody's going to touch Kate, I want the person to be the best, and Jenny can tell us if the surgeon knows what the hell he's doing."

PATRICK GULPED down the bitter hospital coffee and stared sightlessly out the glass window, down into the parking lot below. Kate had been in surgery for hours now, with no word.

Jenny had called Dana on that hellacious ride back through Logan to the regional hospital that served the town. He'd heard Dana lose at least some of her fear as she listened to Jenny. Jenny was doing what Jenny did best—talking in the cool, detached, clinical way that had driven him crazy when Annabelle was sick.

It felt weird and twisted that his ex-wife was talking to Dana. Talking about another little girl he'd come to love.

Dana. At the fountain, he'd made a wish to move on. God, if he could take that wish back. The rational part of him knew Kate's accident wasn't God's answer, but the other part of his mind, the part that kicked himself for having talked Dana into leaving Kate with Lissa and Mel… Had he cost Dana her daughter?

Just give Kate back and I won't bother Dana anymore.

Patrick had been bargaining with God ever since Dana had screamed in the truck. He knew a mother's anguish when he heard it, and in fact, he'd been too busy bargaining to talk to Dana. Just as well. She hadn't been able to form a sentence since they'd gotten back. In the reflection of the glass, he saw her crumpled on a saggy couch in the OR waiting room, gripping Lissa's hand.

Mel was on her other side. Her face was even whiter than Dana's. Her hands were clenched into fists on either side of her knees.

Jenny had gone away, muttering something about getting an update from the OR. Patrick wondered if she'd left to give them space, if she'd felt in the way.

Or had she just been reminded too much of Annabelle.

A glance at the clock showed the second hand sweeping away another minute. Another minute without news. How many times had he stood in a waiting room like this, praying, bargaining, pleading?

He was still here. Still trying to trade his future for a child's.

Give us Kate, and I swear…I swear.

DANA THOUGHT she'd go insane with the waiting. Every time she glanced up to see if Jenny had returned with news, she saw either Patrick's rigid back or Lissa's tear-splotched, guilt-ridden face…or Mel, who hadn't uttered a sound since they'd walked into the room.

Dana had to get out of this waiting room. The walls were closing in on her. On shaky knees, she rose and staggered to the door. A labyrinth of hallways stretched in front of her.

She saw a discreet sign pointing toward a recessed door that proclaimed Chapel, and she headed for the sanctuary. Inside, the room smelled of lemon furniture polish and rose potpourri, far different from the antiseptic odors of the hospital corridor.

It undid her. She fell on her knees at the tiny altar and sobbed. "Oh, God, please, please, this is all my fault. Please—"

The door opened behind her, and a hand touched her shoulder. "No. No, Dana. It's my fault."

She raised eyes blurred with tears to find Mel. The young woman sank beside her. Mel didn't meet Dana's eyes, just fastened them on the open Bible in front of her. "It was my fault. I was arguing with Lissa…about you. And we weren't watching Kate."

Dana was past caring who besides herself was culpable. If she hadn't been on a boat, letting herself get swept away by hormones, Mel wouldn't have been arguing with Lissa. And Kate would have been safe.

"I know you don't want to hear my apology now." Mel's voice was small and quiet. "But it's my fault. I wanted to make Lissa pay. I wanted her…I don't know what I wanted. I wanted her to see that Dad…"

Dana sat back in the pew. "It's okay, Mel. I shouldn't have been with your father in the first place. I had no business doing anything to add to the trouble between you and Lissa. I shouldn't have put you at odds with your dad."

"No! Today was a wake-up call for me." Mel grasped Dana's hands. "I realized I was wrong about you and Dad. Just as I was wrong about Annabelle. All this time it wasn't Dad I was afraid for."

"I don't understand."

Mel let go of Dana's hands and rubbed her palms on her pants. The fabric was blood stained, with Kate's blood, Dana realized with a thud of her heart. Mel was continuing on. "Lissa went to pieces, screaming, shouting. I had to do first aid on Kate. And that's when I realized I hadn't wanted her around…because I was afraid. For me. I was afraid I'd get attached and I'd love her—or any kid."

"Why on earth would you be afraid of that?" Dana was too tired to figure it out.

"Because when I was little, I didn't want Annabelle. I didn't want another baby sister. Lissa already took up so much of my parents' time, and then when Annabelle came along, everybody expected me to be happy I had somebody else to share Mom and Dad with. I didn't want her. I wished…for her not to be there. And then suddenly I didn't have her anymore. It was what I wanted, what I thought I wanted. And somehow, I don't know…" Mel pressed her lips together and put her fingers to her mouth.

"You didn't think you deserved a second chance."

"Sounds crazy when you say it like that. When I realize it now. But I knew, the minute I heard that television topple, the minute I saw Kate lying there—" A strangled cry tore from Mel. "I just want that chance. Whether I deserve it or not. And I don't want you blaming yourself."

"Hard for me not to." She thought about Patrick, how he'd been so crippled emotionally after Annabelle's death. She'd been so demanding, needing him to "move on" in some way so that he would be ready for a relationship with her. And now she'd had a glimpse into the nightmare he'd survived all these years.

"I'm sorry I've been such a—" Mel gestured with upturned palms "—you know. About you and Dad."

Dana took in a deep breath and drew in more of that lemony furniture polish scent. She'd never think of lemons without thinking of this day. "This…relationship? We're not going anywhere, your dad and me. We weren't. He's not ready, and I can understand why."

Mel frowned. "No. He loves you—and Kate. I know that."

"Mel—"

"No, Dana. Trust me. Do you believe for one minute he would have told me to call Mom if he hadn't been ready to do anything in his power for you two? He hasn't spoken to her in years. Not voluntarily, anyway."

Dana held her forehead. "It's not just that. Sometimes more than an attraction, more than love, is required. And besides, I can't think of that now. I have to think of Kate. Not thinking of Kate is what got me here."

"Don't give up on him. Not because of me. Because I was so selfish." A tear trickled down Mel's face.

The door hinges creaked, and Dana and Mel looked up. Jenny stood in the doorway, her face tired. "The surgeon's out here. He's ready to talk to you."

Dana struggled to her feet. Her heart hammered. She tried to read the woman's expression but was too terrified. Mel rose beside her and slipped her hand into Dana's.

"Mom?" Mel's question was choked.

But Jenny didn't answer. She put an arm around Dana and shepherded them toward the door.

Out in the hall, the surgeon waited with Patrick, his scrubs wrinkled, his eyes fatigued. Dana attempted to gauge the news by how he looked as he slumped against the corridor's wall.

"Ms. Wilson?" He straightened. "I'm Dr. Kendall."

Dana attempted to form a question, but the words wouldn't come. "Yes?"

"Peter Kendall, if you drag this out…" Jenny trailed off.

Dr. Kendall quirked an eyebrow. "Still figure you can boss everybody around, Jenny?" His mouth formed a small smile.

He turned to Dana and took her hands in his. "She's okay. Your daughter is okay. The television broke a couple of ribs and punctured a lung, so she has chest tubes in, but she's breathing on her own. We had to remove her spleen, and she's lost a lot of blood. She's got a long, long way to go. This was major surgery, and it takes time for the body to recover its strength after a splenectomy. But we've patched her up and stitched her back together. She's gonna make it."

Dana's knees wouldn't hold her anymore. She sagged onto the floor, burying her face into her hands, and sobbed with relief and joy.

CHAPTER TWENTY-EIGHT

FOR PATRICK, the jubilation of Kate's pulling through faded all too soon into days of gray pain. He'd made a bargain, and this time God had accepted it.

The pain was all the more sharp because he hadn't had to explain it to Dana. Beyond that day at the hospital, when she'd gripped his hands in gratitude, she hadn't called. She hadn't come by.

True, she had her hands full with Kate, who'd only just been released from the hospital. And just as true, he could have dropped by their house. But what was the point? He'd cost one woman a child already. Maybe it was a curse or a jinx, but he couldn't risk it after God had elected to spare Kate.

He had slipped into the hospital a couple of times, late at night, after he hoped Dana would be asleep. Once, Kate had been awake. He hadn't said anything, just put his fingers to his lips. She'd asked him to sing the silly lullaby again, and he had. In the chair beside the bed, Dana had slept on.

Beyond that, he'd managed to stay away. Mel and Lissa nagged him, and at one point refused to give him any more updates. "Dad, if you want to know, you'll just have to go find out yourself," Mel had told him.

She'd also told him that she had found a counselor.

She'd invited him along. "It might help, Dad. Don't be mad with me. I think I need it."

Patrick had remembered the conversation with Luke and how he'd wanted kids. He'd smiled at her. "You go on, Mel. Whatever you think helps, I'm all for it."

Vann had joined the chorus of concerned voices, and today, at the table with the other board-of-education members, he kept casting apprehensive looks Patrick's way.

That could have been because of the letter of resignation Patrick had given him a week earlier, the day Kate had been released from the hospital. Vann had refused to honor the resignation. "If you want to do this, you bring it up at the next meeting."

So here Patrick was, fidgeting with his copy of that letter. No point in putting off the inevitable. He was doing no one any good. Besides, somehow it had leaked out and his plans were common knowledge.

He brought the meeting to order, and they went through the motions of the Pledge of Allegiance and the invocation. For Patrick, these simple routines seemed bittersweet. He wondered if he was doing the right thing.

As he opened his eyes, he gulped. Dana stood just inside the doorway, waiting for the prayer to be done so she could join them.

Seeing her there diminished the earlier ache he'd felt at saying his last Pledge of Allegiance as board chairman. Wanting someone this badly and knowing he wasn't the right man for her was real anguish.

She held a sheaf of papers in her hand. Vann smiled her way as she took a seat in the empty front row.

Was this something that Vann had cooked up? Maybe he believed having Dana here would dissuade Patrick from resigning.

If so, Vann had miscalculated. How could Patrick continue in this job when, because he'd wanted Dana to himself, he'd put Kate in danger? He'd tried to explain this to his friend, but somehow the more he parsed his explanation, the more tangled it became.

Of course, the board didn't have to know all Patrick's reasons for calling the job quits. "Before we begin with the old business, I'd like to—"

Patrick didn't get his prepared speech started. Dana stood up and interrupted. "Uh, I realize I'm not on the agenda. But the superintendent told me that he would give me a few minutes."

Vann nodded. "And Ms. Wilson has a child recovering from surgery, as you well know, Patrick, so if you don't mind…"

What could Patrick say? He surveyed the other board members. Their expressions ranged from mild interest on Gabriella's face to prurient nosiness in Evans's and Curtis's as they leaned forward.

"Okay. Ms. Wilson." He steeled himself for whatever would come next.

Dana stood, the stack of papers quivering in her hands. Patrick noticed the trembling and sent a reproachful glare Vann's way. Vann should have remembered how much Dana loathed public speaking.

She cleared her throat. "First of all, I want to thank you for the time off you've allowed me to be with my daughter. Kate is doing much better, although she's still got a long recovery in front of her—at least another month, the doctors say."

Patrick leaned back in his chair. "We're glad to do it. Anything you need. As long as you need. Right?"

The other board members echoed his sentiments.

He relaxed. Maybe this was solely about Dana's desire to show her gratitude.

The sheaf of papers trembled some more as Dana spoke up again. "I really do appreciate it. And I appreciate the outpouring of support the community has shown me. It's made me realize how special this town is. The people have brought food and flowers and cards...and this." She held up the papers.

Patrick's mouth went dry. "What is that, exactly?"

Dana wasn't looking at him. She had her eyes on Curtis and Evans at the far end of the table, and she crossed over to stand directly in front of them. "This is a petition. It has over five hundred signatures on it." Dana fanned out the pages in front of the board members. "Most of them are from your districts, Mr. Evans and Mr. Curtis. From parents there. And they're asking for a chance to hold a school bond referendum. If the state can provide any money whatsoever to build a new school, these parents are willing to go to bat for a school bond."

Curtis snatched the papers toward him. Together he and Evans examined page after page of signatures. "Is this what you've been doing during your time off? I thought your kid was sick," Evans said.

"Not me." She swept her eyes toward Patrick. "Once the community heard that Patrick was considering re-signing in protest, parents knew they had to step up to the plate. They knew they had to show you that he was right. The community does want a new school."

Curtis pushed away the pages. "How can we be sure these are real signatures, or that the people are even residents of this county?"

Dana's eyes went cold in a way Patrick knew all too well. She reached into her tote bag. "I thought this might be your reaction. So I brought a list of registered voters. And here's a list of elementary school parents, as well." She slapped both lists down on the board table. "A good portion of those five-hundred-plus people are standing outside the building."

Evans sprang from his seat and parted the miniblinds. "There've got to be two hundred people outside!" He whirled. "And all these people are here for a tax *increase?*"

"No. Nobody wants a tax increase," Dana said. "They just want a school badly enough to put up with a tax increase."

Evans's peek out of the window served as a signal. Down the hall, the front door opened, and parents filed in. The room quickly filled. Patrick stared in slack-jawed amazement. He'd never had the faith to carry his cause to the people, but here they were, bringing it to him. He'd always taken at face value that Curtis and Evans knew what the majority of their districts wanted.

And he'd been wrong.

Vann gave him a discreet thumbs-up. Patrick rubbed his jaw, trying to decide the best and most diplomatic way to proceed.

But Curtis beat him to it. He addressed the crowd. "Anybody here *not* want a referendum on the school bond?"

Except for some shuffling feet and rustling jackets, the room remained silent. Curtis turned to Evans. "I see a lot of folks from my district. Connor, is this one of your stunts? You dream this up?"

Patrick shook his head. "I knew nothing about it."

Curtis picked up the petition again, paged through it. "I guess the people have spoken. I make a motion to at least have a referendum on a school bond to build a new elementary school."

The crowd erupted in thunderous applause. Patrick almost didn't hear the second to the motion that had failed so many times in the past. As he brought the measure to a full vote, he spotted Dana slipping from the room.

The voting finished, he made a motion for a recess and plunged through the throng after her.

He found her at her car. "Dana. Thank you. I don't know how you did it, but thank you."

"No, Patrick. Thank *you*." She gazed across the roof of her car, her hand on the door handle. "Asking Jenny to help, stepping in and be there when I wasn't had to be hard. But you did it. My appearance here—well, it's my way of showing you how much I appreciate what you did."

"Vann told you, didn't he? That I was planning to resign."

"You told me, remember? Vann just told me you'd made it official. You shouldn't quit. If you're quitting because of me, don't worry. I have to get Kate through this, so that means I have to hang on to this job for the insurance. But just as soon as she's back on her feet, I'm leaving."

His breath caught. He came around the car to stand beside her. "I wasn't quitting because of you. Well, not exactly."

Sorrow twisted her features. "It's okay, Patrick. I understand."

"No. You don't. You couldn't."

She brushed his shoulder. "I do. I realized what I was asking of you the day Kate was hurt. I finally got it. If Kate had died…"

"What happened to Kate wasn't your fault. Don't blame yourself. If it was anybody's fault, it was mine." Patrick swallowed. "If I could have explained to you…if I could have just talked with you the way you'd wanted me to, you would have never wanted to be around me. And then Kate wouldn't have gotten hurt."

She cocked her head. "Patrick, what on earth could you have said to me to make me not want to be around you?"

He closed his eyes, gritted his teeth against the pain and the guilt. "It was my fault."

"That Kate got hurt? No. It was an accident."

"No. That Annabelle died."

"Oh, Patrick. No. You can't control cancer." Dana tried to take his hand, but he couldn't bear her touch.

"I wanted a boy." The confession, and the tears that it evoked, strangled him. But once he'd let those words loose, the release couldn't be held back. "Jenny was happy. We had two girls. A family of four, a white picket fence. It was enough, plus she had her med school to finish. But I held out. I wheedled. And I begged. I wanted one more shot at a boy to go fishing with. To be a quarterback. To follow in my footsteps."

He dragged in a breath. Dana wasn't saying anything. He couldn't tell from her face whether she was silent out of disgust or whether she was simply letting him talk.

Patrick plunged on. "And finally, one day, she just said, 'Well, okay, one more kid. But girl or boy, that's it.'"

"Annabelle." Dana's whisper was barely audible.

"Annabelle." He wiped at his eyes, desperate not to cry. "The minute I held her in my arms, I didn't care a flying fig that she'd never play football. She was mine. She was my angel."

"That's all that matters—"

"No. No, dammit. Don't you see? If I hadn't wanted a boy, she would have never been born and then she wouldn't—" Now, despite his best effort, a tear streaked down his face.

"Oh, God, Patrick, no. You can't think that way." Dana wrapped her arms around him. "She was yours. She was yours for as long as God saw fit to loan her to you. And you can't tell me that your life wasn't richer for knowing her. You can't tell me you would have been better off if she hadn't been born. She made you who you are. She made you the man I love."

He stood there trembling and jerking in her arms, undone, unmanned and uncaring who saw. Dana loved him. Despite what he was, despite his failings. She loved him.

Patrick set her back from him and stared at her. She stared back, unflinching. "What?" she asked.

"Will you wait for me?"

"Wait?"

"If I can get my head screwed on straight, will you and Kate wait for me? You make me whole. You make this ache in me bearable, somehow. You make me brave in ways I never thought I could be."

Dana scrubbed away her own tears with the heel of her hand. She nodded. "I'll wait. But you can't quit."

"You can't, either. Don't you and Kate leave me."

"I'm here." Dana reached up and kissed him, then broke off the kiss to tell him, "I'm here to stay."

* * * * *

Silhouette Desire kicks off 2009 with
MAN OF THE MONTH, *a yearlong program*
featuring incredible heroes by stellar authors.

When navy SEAL Hunter Cabot returns home
for some much needed R and R, he discovers he's
a married man. There's just one problem: he's
never met his "bride."

Enjoy this sneak peek at Maureen Child's
AN OFFICER AND A MILLIONAIRE.
Available January 2009 from Silhouette Desire.

One

Hunter Cabot, Navy SEAL, had a healing bullet wound in his side, thirty days' leave and, apparently, a wife he'd never met.

On the drive into his hometown of Springville, California, he stopped for gas at Charlie Evans's service station. That's where the trouble started.

"Hunter! Man, it's good to see you! Margie didn't tell us you were coming home."

"Margie?" Hunter leaned back against the front fender of his black pickup truck and winced as his side gave a small twinge of pain. Silently then, he watched as the man he'd known since high school filled his tank.

Charlie grinned, shook his head and pumped gas. "Guess your wife was lookin' for a little 'alone' time with you, huh?"

"My—" Hunter couldn't even say the word. *Wife?* He didn't have a wife. "Look, Charlie"

"Don't blame her, of course," his friend said with a wink as he finished up and put the gas cap back on. "You being gone all the time with the SEALs must be hard on the ol' love life."

He'd never had any complaints, Hunter thought, frowning at the man still talking a mile a minute. "What're you—"

"Bet Margie's anxious to see you. She told us all about that R and R trip you two took to Bali." Charlie's dark brown eyebrows lifted and wiggled.

"Charlie…"

"Hey, it's okay, you don't have to say a thing, man."

What the hell could he say? Hunter shook his head, paid for his gas and as he left, told himself Charlie was just losing it. Maybe the guy had been smelling gas fumes too long.

But as it turned out, it wasn't just Charlie. Stopped at a red light on Main Street, Hunter glanced out his window to smile at Mrs. Harker, his second-grade teacher who was now at least a hundred years old. In the middle of the crosswalk, the old lady stopped and shouted, "Hunter Cabot, you've got yourself a wonderful wife. I hope you appreciate her."

Scowling now, he only nodded at the old woman— the only teacher who'd ever scared the crap out of him. What the hell was going on here? Was everyone but him nuts?

His temper beginning to boil, he put up with a few more comments about his "wife" on the drive through town before finally pulling into the wide, circular drive leading to the Cabot mansion. Hunter didn't have a clue what was going on, but he planned to get to the bottom of it. Fast.

He grabbed his duffel bag, stalked into the house and paid no attention to the housekeeper, who ran at him, fluttering both hands. "Mr. Hunter!"

"Sorry, Sophie," he called out over his shoulder as he took the stairs two at a time. "Need a shower, then we'll talk."

He marched down the long, carpeted hallway to the rooms that were always kept ready for him. In his suite,

Hunter tossed the duffel down and stopped dead. The shower in his bathroom was running. His *wife?*

Anger and curiosity boiled in his gut, creating a churning mass that had him moving forward without even thinking about it. He opened the bathroom door to a wall of steam and the sound of a woman singing—off-key. Margie, no doubt.

Well, if she was his wife… Hunter walked across the room, yanked the shower door open and stared in at a curvy, naked, temptingly wet woman.

She whirled to face him, slapping her arms across her naked body while she gave a short, terrified scream.

Hunter smiled. "Hi, honey. I'm home."

* * * * *

Be sure to look for
AN OFFICER AND A MILLIONAIRE
by USA TODAY *bestselling author Maureen Child.*
Available January 2009 from Silhouette Desire.

CELEBRATE
60 YEARS
OF PURE READING PLEASURE
WITH HARLEQUIN®!

We'll be spotlighting a different series
every month throughout 2009
to celebrate our 60th anniversary.
Look for Silhouette Desire® in January!

Collect all 12 books in the Silhouette Desire®
Man of the Month continuity, starting in
January 2009 with *An Officer and a Millionaire*
by *USA TODAY* bestselling author
Maureen Child.

*Look for one new Man of the Month title
every month in 2009!*

REQUEST YOUR FREE BOOKS!

2 FREE NOVELS PLUS 2 FREE GIFTS!

® HARLEQUIN®

Super Romance®

Exciting, emotional, unexpected!

YES! Please send me 2 FREE Harlequin Superromance® novels and my 2 FREE gifts (gifts are worth about $10). After receiving them, if I don't wish to receive any more books, I can return the shipping statement marked "cancel." If I don't cancel, I will receive 6 brand-new novels every month and be billed just $4.69 per book in the U.S. or $5.24 per book in Canada, plus 25¢ shipping and handling per book and applicable taxes, if any*. That's a savings of close to 15% off the cover price! I understand that accepting the 2 free books and gifts places me under no obligation to buy anything. I can always return a shipment and cancel at any time. Even if I never buy another book from Harlequin, the two free books and gifts are mine to keep forever.

135 HDN EEX7 336 HDN EEYK

Name	(PLEASE PRINT)
Address	Apt. #
City	State/Prov.	Zip/Postal Code

Signature (if under 18, a parent or guardian must sign)

Mail to the **Harlequin Reader Service:**
IN U.S.A.: P.O. Box 1867, Buffalo, NY 14240-1867
IN CANADA: P.O. Box 609, Fort Erie, Ontario L2A 5X3

Not valid to current subscribers of Harlequin Superromance books.

Want to try two free books from another line?
Call 1-800-873-8635 or visit www.morefreebooks.com.

* Terms and prices subject to change without notice. N.Y. residents add applicable sales tax. Canadian residents will be charged applicable provincial taxes and GST. Offer not valid in Quebec. This offer is limited to one order per household. All orders subject to approval. Credit or debit balances in a customer's account(s) may be offset by any other outstanding balance owed by or to the customer. Please allow 4 to 6 weeks for delivery. Offer available while quantities last.

Your Privacy: Harlequin is committed to protecting your privacy. Our Privacy Policy is available online at www.eHarlequin.com or upon request from the Reader Service. From time to time we make our lists of customers available to reputable third parties who may have a product or service of interest to you. If you would prefer we not share your name and address, please check here. ☐

HSR08R

USA TODAY BESTSELLING AUTHOR

TARA
TAYLOR
QUINN

A woman, a judge—a target

Criminal court judge Hannah Montgomery is presiding over a
murder trial. When the jury finds the defendant, Bobby Donahue,
not guilty, Hannah's convinced they've reached the wrong verdict.
Especially when strange things start happening around her...

AT CLOSE
RANGE

*Available the first week
of December 2008,
wherever paperbacks
are sold!*

"An exceptionally powerful book."
—*Booklist* on *Behind Closed Doors*

COMING NEXT MONTH